COMPARED TO WHAT

SABIN PRENTIS

This is a work of fiction. All names, characters, places, and incidents are the product of the author's imagination. Any resemblance to real events or persons, living or dead, is entirely coincidental.

© 2019 Sabin Prentis Duncan

Published by Fielding Books, Richmond, VA

ISBN - 13: 978-0-9984885-3-0

*To my late mother, Joanne Duncan,
and every woman who strived to make a difference only to feel that
their efforts were for naught.
You are loved, valued, and appreciated.*

*Additionally, I want to thank and note that inspiration for this novel
is derived from the mentorship and examples provided by Jovita
Davis, Rosalannd Daley, Laverne Mingus, Jerilyn Cross, Gilda
Myles, Marybeth Hefner, Joe Guillen, and Julius Maddox.*

AUTHOR'S NOTE

This book is both a prequel and sequel to the previously released, *Better Left Unsaid*.

Hopefully, you choose to enjoy them both.

Thank you for your support.

Much love,
Sabin Prentis

"The race is not given to the swift nor the strong,
but they who endureth 'til the end!"

— *JOANNE DUNCAN'S PARAPHRASE OF*
ECCLESIASTES 9:11

I STAND ACCUSED

Isaac Hayes

September 1, 2013

*S*chool Crooks.

That was the headline of the Detroit newspaper. Beneath the caption were two large color photos. The photo on the left was of Richard Gilliam, the Chief Financial Officer of A New Way Charter Schools, and the one on the right was of Elaine Robeson, Principal of Ella Baker Academy.

Both were charged with misappropriating funds. Mr. Gilliam's responsibility over the finances of all five A New Way Charter Schools provided ample opportunity for his swindling of over a million dollars in a three year span for personal use. Three years of Red Wings season ticket seats just behind the glass partition, a recently purchased, fully-furnished home in Michigan's Upper Peninsula, and other smaller personal trappings - a Rolex and a new red Lincoln Navigator - were evidence of Richard's clandestine accounting practices. While he vowed to fight the charges in court, Mr. Gilliam's attorney's highest optimism lay in a gray area of hope between a plea bargain or some type of protracted restitution plan that would keep Richard out of prison.

The case against Principal Robeson was an entirely different matter.

In a two year span, Principal Robeson intentionally redirected nearly four hundred thousand dollars from technology related purchases toward hiring an additional teacher and sponsoring a catered weekend breakfast and tutorial program for the families of her impoverished students. Principal Robeson did not profit from her activity; yet in the court of public opinion, she was being vilified as Richard's co-conspirator or worse, his puppet.

The *school crooks* label cut Elaine deeply. The newspaper article was featured prominently on the Sunday edition preceding Labor Day. Turning the Robeson family holiday cookout into a solemn affair. Shortly after reading the headlines, Elaine was notified at home that she would be placed on administrative leave while an investigation ensued. Having her character besmirched publicly without an opportunity to defend herself was traumatic. Even more traumatizing was the separation of Elaine from a source of personal satisfaction - serving the families of Detroit.

The thought that people would question, doubt, or judge her commitment to children and families pushed Elaine over the cliff of disappointment into the abysmal valley of despondency. A valley of which she was familiar, having traversed its terrain following the arrest and imprisonment of her daughter. It took years of navigating the valley's thick grey clouds of depression to begin scaling the mountainside of hope. Elaine knew the valley of despondency well; only this time, she was not sure she wanted to leave.

AIN'T NO WAY

Aretha Franklin

September 1, 2013

"Mama, that's bullshit. Them newspaper people can't do you like that! Who in the hell do they think they are? After all you've done for them kids and ..."

"Song. baby please." Elaine exhaled slowly, the pain was too new. That Songhai would call was assuring, even loving. But Elaine really wasn't ready to talk about the newspaper article or its implications. Quite simply, she needed to catch her breath, before she imploded.

"Song, call me later this week. Looks like I'm going to have some extra time on my hands so I'll be out to see you on Friday. I love you."

"Mama, no! Don't hang up. We gotta fuck those people up! They can't just be lying on you and making up shit. You didn't steal no money! Mama, we need to ..."

"SONG! baby please!" Elaine counted to five before continuing. "Song, I appreciate your support. Baby, just give me ..." Elaine's voice was cracking. "Give me a chance to sort this mess out, ok? See you Monday, alright?"

Songhai let out a sigh of surrender. Her anger hadn't subsided but she did not want to add any additional strain onto her mother. Plus, didn't she just say Friday and then Monday?

"Mama?"

"Yes, baby?"

"You said Friday and then you said Monday. Can you come on Friday?"

"Oh, yes, baby. Friday, I meant Friday. I love you baby. Alright now, talk to you later."

"Ok mama, I love you too."

Song hated to hang up.

"You finished wit' yo' call? You ain't the only one who gotta talk to they peoples," a gruff-voiced, overly-tattooed inmate said menacingly. Song abruptly bumped her shoulder against the woman as she passed. She ignored the woman's comments as she was preoccupied with worry over her mother.

"Yeah bitch. You betta walk away," the inmate said to the back of Song's head.

ELAINE HELD THE PHONE IN ITS PLACE ON THE RECEIVER and reflected on her daughter, her fiery spirit, and willingness to fight. Both Song and Stokely, Elaine's son, were fighters. But with Song, it was such a surprise. Songhai was gorgeous, intelligent, and just down right sweet. Yet, her sweetness could turn to spitfire if someone called her "Red." Song despised the nickname and thought it demeaning. The orangish tint on her brown complexion and dark red hair made it easy to see why the "Red" nickname would come to someone's mind. But Song was emphatic that she be addressed by her name, Songhai, which acknowledged her womanhood and her culture. Elaine realized that the fierceness she occasionally displayed as a child had become her dominant personality in prison. Then Elaine imagined she would need to acquire a similar veneer of toughness to proceed through the ordeal that lay ahead. That is, if she chooses to proceed.

"MAMA! WHERE YOU AT?" STOKELY SHOUTED.

"Boy, quit all that hollering! I'm in the backroom."

Every Sunday preceding Labor Day, Elaine and her husband, Cleve, short for Cleveland, hosted fifteen to twenty of their closest friends and family. Following the processing of that morning's newspaper, Cleve had been busy calling guests to inform them that there would be no cookout at the Robeson's this year. He had reached everyone except their son, Stokely, who arrived soon after Cleve made the last call.

"Ma? Dad said you were having a tough morning. Is there anything I can do to make it better?"

Elaine was seated in her favorite seat by the window with a view of the backyard. When her eyes met Stokely's, her gaze held a dispiriting mix of sadness and anger. She extended her hand with the newspaper to Stokely.

"You haven't seen the paper, have you?"

Stokely, taken aback by his mother's moroseness, slowly shook his head 'No' while reaching for the paper. He took it without taking his eyes off his mother. As she nodded to him as if to say 'Go on,' he looked at the headline and gasped.

Unlike every other weekend which found Stokely with an abundance of free time, on this day, Stokely was accompanied by his girlfriend, Tanya. Elaine admired Tanya in a woman-to-woman way, but something just didn't sit right when she looked at Tanya as her son's love interest. Typically, Tanya traveled every weekend. Elaine was incredulous at the thought of all the weekends to be available, Tanya would be in town this weekend. Elaine wasn't in the mood to be a hostess to anyone today. She wanted to be alone.

After sitting on the love-seat sofa a few feet away from his mother, Stokely read the newspaper. Moments later, he remarked, "The allegations against you are thin at best. They have this picture of you as if you and this Gilliam were co-conspirators; but, the overwhelming majority of the article details his activity. The two paragraphs about you come across as hearsay and speculation."

Then pointing to the photos of documents from Richard's accounting files, "See they are parading evidence against him and mentioning you as an afterthought. No way any judge would act on such flimsy gossip."

Elaine sighed before replying, "I hope it never reaches a judge."

Stokely was about to say something and stopped as if something were lodged in his throat. He pondered a second as he contemplated what he thought he heard behind his mother's words. He softened his voice a bit before adding, "Mama, you're going to fight this aren't you?"

Elaine allowed her gaze to fix upon a small black squirrel scurrying up a tree. She thought that though the squirrel is black, it belongs to the grey squirrel species. The squirrel is technically grey while it appears black. What the squirrel is and what it appears to be are different. "How fitting," she thought as she replayed her anxieties about her career and the allegations made by the newspaper.

3

HOLD ON, I'M COMIN'

Sam & Dave

Sunday, September 1, 2013

*C*leve was putting the finishing touches on a pair of sandwiches he intended to share with his wife, when Elaine and her pervading cloud of doom entered the kitchen.

To described her as broken-spirited would have been an optimistic description.

She ambled over to Cleve's open arms and as soon as her forehead hit his chest, a loud sobbing, "Why?" escaped her throat.

Cleve wrapped her in his arms and squeezed her tight. He evoked a paternal, soothing, side-to-side rocking while whispering, "'Laine, we gonna get through this, baby. We're gonna do it."

While Cleve is a man of many endeavors, his bread and butter revenue source is plumbing. Like most veteran plumbers, Cleve's hands were large, calloused, and strong. With those hands, he gripped both of Elaine's arms and lifted her to a seat on the countertop.

In most instances, the idea of a man putting his hands on

a woman evokes fear; yet, Elaine had long recognized the irony and felt as safe as she did the first time Cleve put his hands on her.

Tuesday, July 25, 1967

SHIT WAS BAD.

That was the description the foreman used to describe what was going on in the streets and why Cleve could anticipate Dodge Main being closed for the next few days.

The leader of their assembly line team, also recommended that Cleve "Get-on outta town and visit some family, 'cause dis shit liable to be much worse fo' it get much better."

Moments later, Cleve threw a packed bag into the back-seat of his Deuce & a Quarter and figured he would drive west on Clairmount, swing over to Joy Road, keep on going to Grand River to Telegraph, and then take that north out of the city. Amid the chaotic climate, one image with a frightening backdrop prompted Cleve to swing hard to the curb and jump out his car.

In the distance, perhaps a block and half north, the U.S. National Guard troops and a tank were proceeding southward on Linwood Ave. Closer to where Cleve pulled over was a young lady with a satchel of rocks, standing in the middle of the street as if she were going to take on the National Guard alone.

"Sista, what the hell you doing?!" he shouted as he approached her from the side and grabbed her arm that was cocked and ready to throw a rock.

She tried to shrug his grip while shouting, "Y'all can't have our city!"

Cleve snatched her and her satchel of rocks.

She struggled and managed to toss one rock feebly. However, the fear that was overtaking Cleve steeled his strength in such a way that he lifted her squirming body and shoved her into the open driver's door of his car.

She was still shouting a diatribe about racist pigs.

He shoved her over to the passenger side, slammed the door, and leapt away from the curb.

"Gotdamn girl!" he shouted as his heart raced and he steered onto Joy Road.

She was panting heavily as she scooted against the door. With her satchel in her lap and her hand gripping another rock, she stared indignantly at Cleve.

His co-worker's words had pressed him into action, but the seeing the troops and this girl with her damn rocks, catapulted his adrenaline into overdrive. He was driving more franticly than bank robbers during a getaway. His turn onto Grand River was done with squealing tires and a racing heart.

She just stared.

LIKE NOW, THROUGH A FOG OF SADNESS, ELAINE STARED AT Cleve.

Most who knew Elaine envisioned her as a combination of Marva Collins and Joe Clark - strength, wisdom, courage, and tough love all rolled into one. Her thirty-five year career as a teacher and administrator with Detroit Public Schools had created for her a type of cult following of former students, parents, and community leaders who believed in and trusted her. When some people lament about what went wrong with Detroit Public Schools, they point to the departure of proven committed leaders like Elaine as the tipping point. However, her foray into charter school administration did not dull her commitment to serving students, teachers, staff, and families. In fact, the new organizational structure gave her more leadership latitude, more influence, and more control. Pessimists would argue that greater control is what got her in the mess she is in.

But Cleve isn't a pessimist.

He is a protector.

With his wife perched on the countertop sniffling like a sad child, Cleve very gently used his thumb to wipe the tears escaping his wife's eyes. Then he gripped her shoulders in a way as to straighten her up. Leaned closer and with lips and noses nearly touching, peered through Elaine's sadness fog and into her eyes.

"Ever since I met you, you been fightin'. Ain't no use in you stoppin' now."

As her chin sunk to her chest, Cleve caught it with his knuckle and lifted her head so that her eyes met his.

"Get yo' rocks ready, Laine; we got a whole army to fight."

4

WHAT'S GOING ON?

Marvin Gaye

Friday, October 25, 2013

"*R*eporting from the Frank Murphy Hall of Justice, we are joined by Attorney Laverne Mankiller and Principal Elaine Robeson. Moments ago, Judge Motley ruled on the two charter school administrators accused of money mismanagement. Former Chief Financial Officer Richard Gilliam will have to post bail and stand trial for his role in stealing money from A New Way Charter Schools. However, Judge Connie Motley has dismissed the case against Principal Robeson. Listen to Judge Motley's statement:"

> On the surface, it appears that Principal Robeson disregarded the trust placed in her by the school board and the management company. However, none of the evidence shows that she profited or that the monies in question were not used for the benefit of the students. The case against Principal Robeson is a human resource matter and should be handled by the Ella Baker Academy School Board and A New Way Charter Schools Management Company.

"Attorney Mankiller, what is your client's response to the ruling?"

"Both Principal Robeson and I believe that Judge Motley's ruling is fair and correct. We look forward to presenting our case to the school board."

"Thank you, Attorney Mankiller. Principal Robeson, how do you feel about the public sentiment that A New Way Charter Schools is rehashing the old way money was managed in DPS."

"My client has no comment but will address concerns during the school board hearings."

"And there you have it from the Frank Murphy Hall of Justice, one administrator found guilty and the other still awaiting her fate."

CLEVE TURNED DOWN THE VOLUME ON THE TV.

Elaine sat stoically.

In an attempt to lighten the mood, Stokely chimed in, "Ma, you look like you're ready to fight. Don't seem like you're scared of nothing."

His comment garnered a brief smile from his mother. In an effort to keep the humor going, Stokely added, "Dad, you standing back there like the Fruit of Islam!"

Cleve let loose a loud laughter that prompted Elaine to laugh a bit. Then he added, "Can't have my baby out dere fighting this thang solo. Shoot between me and Mankiller, we gonna see this thang through."

"Yeah, looks like Mankiller is the right lawyer for Ma's case," Stokely added.

"Ain't gonna be no case when we get finish with the facts. See they ain't saying the whole truth. They trying to bundle up 'Laine with that crook, Gilliam, but he ain't never been 'bout the people."

Cleve's protectiveness was getting riled, which caused Elaine to lean into his shoulder to temper its intensity. Reflexively, he wrapped his arm around her shoulder and pulled her closer.

Stokely and Cleve's conversation continued as Elaine's thoughts became further entrenched within her spirit. She just couldn't bring herself to say much. Of all the heartache and disappointments she has endured – from her daughter's imprisonment to even way back to her abandonment as a child – this public spectacle of lies and distorted truths has gutted her soul. She has been a faithful and damn good educator for over forty years and this is her reward? Being slandered like a thief. How could anyone believe those lies?

They were watching the 6 o'clock news and its re-airing of this morning's lead-in story. However, when Cleve changed the channel, the local Fox News station had its own spin on the case.

Stokely verbalized his parent's feelings when the images of Armstrong Thomas and Reverend Amos Thigpen flashed before them, "These fools right here ..."

Elaine took the remote and turned up the mini-press conference held by two of the five Ella Baker Academy school board members. To her, the sight of those two was repulsive and sickening.

The press conference began with Thomas, a former aide in President Bush's administration and who some Detroiters thought was a white-folks Negro, a black face advancing an imperialist agenda.

Everything about Armstrong Thomas was forgettable. His features were neither handsome nor unattractive, they were just so. His size was neither imposing nor underwhelming, it was just so. His attire was neither flamboyant nor cheap, it was just so. Privately, Elaine had nicknamed him Luke Warm, as he always aimed for the middle and would not take a stand on anything.

His first comments were, "What we have with Principal Robeson is a blessing and a curse. For years, she has served this city and at least to my knowledge, within the last year, chosen to forgo all of that good will to pursue an agenda of her own. The Ella Baker School Board will hold a series of special meetings to address the former Principal Robeson's activities and we will act swiftly to restore the trust of the city in our great school."

Elaine, Cleve, and Stokely, simultaneously rolled their eyes and exhaled sighs that said, "Bullshit." Luke Warm lived up to his moniker.

Reverend Thigpen took the podium.

In his dreams, Reverend Thigpen was a modern manifestation of Reverend C.L. Franklin. Some likened him to an ambulance chasing lawyer because whenever there was an incident covered by news cameras, Reverend Thigpen was present. Others viewed him with ambivalence as he was the go-to Black minister who would stand by the side of a police officer, public official, or other perpetrator of ill will and act as the African American spokesperson and forgiver of the transgressor. He began nearly every statement with bastardized interpretations of bible verses that proved to be polished bullshit but when delivered with Thigpen's Baptist ministerial inflections, sounded authentic.

Usually, when Elaine debriefed Cleve on board meetings, she referred to Reverend Thigpen as the Charlatan of the Cloth.

Luke Warm and the Charlatan of the Cloth were her nemeses and they were vilifying her publicly.

The Charlatan gripped the edges of the podium and looked side to side while furrowing his brow and pursuing his lips. He began with a slow, deliberate cadence.

"The Ella Baker Academy opened in the fall of 2009 committed to carrying forth the Lord's challenge of 'casting our buckets where we are sown.'" Thigpen then took his handkerchief and wiped his upper lip before casting a saddened gaze into the camera. He continued, "In good faith, we followed Gawd's inclinations and chose 'the least of these' in the administrative form of Elaine Robeson."

Thigpen tucked his chin and peered over his glasses.

"We thought we had se-CURED the SER-vices of a community advocate, a GEN-UU-WINE educator, and a servant of the Lawd." Each time he emphasized a syllable, he extended his hand and shook his fingers. Then he balled his fingers into a fist and clutched it tightly into his chest as he added, "But DEE-Troit, we was DE-ceived!" He looked around again. "We was BAM-BOOzled!" He looked over his shoulder at Thomas. Then with fire followed by a slow unwinding almost-whisper, he added, "WE WERE ... led ... astray."

"Now, I don't know WHAT ... former Principal Robeson was thinking when she IN-TEN-TION-ALLY redirected the chillun's money to do her own bidding. But aaaaahhh, Detroit, I do know ..." At this point, he patted the podium top with an open palm, "We will work together to do right by the STU-dents of Ella Baker."

Thomas added an "Amen."

Thigpen rattled on, "For where one or two are gathered in MY NAME, so shall justice be for the chillun' of Detroit." With that, he closed his portfolio and stormed from the stage, leaving Thomas to take questions from the press.

THE ROBESON'S WATCHED THE PRESS CONFERENCE IN horrific disbelief. Cleve added, "These muthafuckas done lost they damn minds."

The news cut away from the press conference and back to the studio where the veteran newscaster, shifted from reporter to editorialist. "With a White House aide and a clergyman on the case, I am sure justice will be served for the Ella Baker students."

Stokely shouted at the screen, "Who the fuck are you?"

"Stokely Medgar Robeson," Elaine replied, "Since when do we curse in front of our mamas?"

Stokely looked at the screen, back at Elaine, at Cleve, and back to Elaine. "I'm sorry Ma." He then looked to the floor before looking back at both his parents, "But they lying on you Ma. What's up with that?"

Cleve chimed in, "That's why we got Mankiller on the case. She gonna cut through all that smoke and mirrors and let the truth be known."

Elaine added with a bit of exasperation, "Yeaaaahhhh, we'll see."

She rose from the sofa and left the room. Cleve and Stokely exchanged looks of concern.

5

I CAN'T GET NEXT TO YOU

The Temptations

Tuesday July 25, 1967

*A*fter slowing to the speed limit and progressing north west along Grand River, Cleve's heartbeat returned to its normal pace. After nearly ten minutes of silence and Elaine burning holes in the side of his face with her glare, Cleve broke the silence.

"You hungry?"

They were approaching Telegraph Road and he wasn't quite sure what he would do with his passenger.

Elaine shifted in her seat and dropped a rock to the floorboard. As she reached to retrieve it, she mumbled, "Yeah."

He hit his turn signal as he approached the intersection. He hung a left and made it a block and half before parking at a small greasy spoon diner. When he turned off the motor, he leaned his head back into the seat and exhaled a deep sigh.

A few seconds passed before he looked to Elaine and with gentle urging, "C'mon lets get a burger or two." He paused and then added, "Who knows, maybe a lil' food will help you throw your rocks farther."

What felt like an enduring silence was broken by the giggle that escaped Elaine.

A slight smile crossed Cleve's face as he exited his side. He hurried over to get the door before Elaine had fully exited.

"Thank you, sir."

"Aww c'mon now with the sir stuff, sister." Cleve laughed. Once he closed her door and extended his hand for a shake. "My name is Cleveland, but er'body just calls me, Cleve." Elaine shook his hand without sharing her name. Cleve pulled slightly before releasing her hand from the shake to get her to head toward the door of the restaurant. He continued his light banter.

"Now if you think Cleveland's an unusual name for a guy living in Detroit, just wait 'till you meet my brother, Columbus."

Elaine paused to face him. "Your name is Cleveland and your brother's name is Columbus?"

Cleve shook his head with a humored expression as they made their way to the booth.

"Is your mother's name Cincinnati or something?"

Cleve clapped his hands and then pointed excitedly at her, "I knew you had a sense of humor!"

Elaine only managed to suppress half her smile as Cleve started talking, "Ma 'Dear wanted to leave the South and thought Ohio was the Promise Land."

Before the waitress could speak, Cleve stated without taking his eyes off Elaine, "Two coffees, please."

The view from the window reveled plumes of smoke in the distance which held the attention of them both until the waitress returned.

6

WHO CAN I RUN TO?

The Jones Girls

Later Friday, October 25, 2013

*B*efore answering her ringing cell phone, Elaine knew who was calling.

And much like their numerous conversations in the past, Francine would commence to talking before Elaine or Joyce could say anything. The advent of three-way calling has been an enduring blessing to their decades-long friendship as it facilitated their frequent sister-girl talks. Talks that began when they were freshmen at Wilberforce University and served as the glue to their bonded sisterhood.

"That damned Thigpen talking shit again!" Francine bellowed as soon as Elaine answered.

Her ferocity was undercut by Joyce's warmer greeting, "Elaine, how you holding up sis?"

A handful of years after they graduated, Cleve dubbed the trio Earth, Wind, and Fire. To him and many others, Joyce was the one who kept the trio grounded, she was the earth. If one were to thumb through some older editions of the thesaurus, Francine would be listed as a synonym for belligerent, thus making her the wind. Elaine was the fire, the advocate for change and the fighter. Years have proven that Cleve was spot-on with the trio's moniker and after Thigpen and Thomas' press conference, the wind and the earth were prepared to help preserve the fire.

"Joyce ..." Elaine paused, "I've been ..." another pause, "Better."

"Damn girl, where in the hell is your spunk? I ain't heard you sound this bad since Marvin Gaye was assassinated!" Francine added.

"Tell Cleve to get you ready, we're coming to get you," Joyce shared.

"I ain't too sure I'm ready to get got," Elaine intoned with mild defeat.

"Aw fuck that shit Elaine! Look what is it? 6:25. Shit, hell, me and Joyce gonna be there by seven." Francine declared.

A declaration the prompted the heartiest laugh of the day from Elaine, "Seven?!"

Joyce then took the conversation baton, "Francine, honey, you know you can't be dressed that fast."

Francine took the jib in-stride as she continued, "I'mma put on my hoodie and we can ride down on yo' boy, Pastor Charlatan!!"

They knew she was sincere, but their years of friendship proved that the 6:25 to 7:00 turn around time for Francine to get ready to go anywhere bordered on impossible. However, to keep Elaine laughing, Joyce added, "Girl get your Timberlands too, so we can stomp out the bullshit."

"STOMP THAT SHIT OUT! Now that's what I'm saying! Fuck Reverend and that tight-assed Thomas! Look Elaine, we gonna be there by 8:00."

Joyce and Elaine continued to laugh before Elaine replied, "Alright, I'll let Cleve know that y'all coming."

"Tell 'em, ain't nobody talking that shit 'bout my girl, now, hell nawl! Tell Cleve we gonna be pulling up about 8:30!"

The laughter continued as they wrapped up their call.

7

HOME IS WHERE THE HATRED IS

Gil Scott-Heron

Tuesday July 25, 1967

"*L*ooks like I'mma need to be getting you home fo' it get too dark." Cleve wiped his mouth with a napkin, then added, "Plus they talkin' 'bout some kinda curfew or something." He looked into Elaine's eyes which were deep pools of nothingness.

He tried something else, "'Bout how far you stay from round here? I mean, where yo' folks live?"

He had grown so accustomed to her short or non-answers that he was a little surprised when she replied, "I ain't got no folks."

Cleve wanted to react but chose to play it cool.

Elaine took the last bite of her second burger and stared out the window at the smoke plumes in the distance.

There was no cadence to her delivery. Her verbalizations were detached from conversation, almost random in response. "I live everywhere and nowhere."

Cleve joined her stare out the window. He sensed her

sporadic speech had some type of purpose and choose to ride it out.

"I mean, last few nights I been staying with Sister Mae. She nice and all but she ain't really family. It's almost like she takes pity on me."

Elaine gulped her cold coffee.

"But at least I can depend on her better than my parents." She then looked directly at Cleve. "You go to church?"

Cleve was rattled. "Well, you know, HEY! I mean, every few Sundays or so, you know I kinda you know shoot the Lord a play."

Elaine didn't really hear him. "My father is a pastor. Somewhere down in Arkansas."

Cleve just nodded slowly.

"My mother ..." Elaine's voice trailed off before she resumed. "My mother was fifteen when she had me." Elaine nodded her head in a begrudging yes motion and said, "The church folks said she was fast and doing the work of the devil by tempting the pastor."

Cleve was confused but thought better of interrupting.

"Can you believe they had a damn Restoration Service where a bunch of preachers prayed for my father so that he can resume leading the church. Meanwhile, my mother was sent to Detroit to have me before she returned back to Arkansas."

"Well, I won't be taking you to their house tonight," Cleve inserted.

"Neither one of my parents raised me. I've just been shuffled from this cousin to that aunt to that neighbor, I mean this shit is so fucking unfair!"

Elaine's raised voice garnered glances from the two other patrons, the waitress, and the cook.

Their stares were oblivious to her. She continued, "That's why I'm getting the hell outta here now that I graduated."

As softly as he could, Cleve asked, "Where you going?"

"Wilberforce."

Cleve laughed and Elaine shot him an evil glare.

"See I told you Ma'Dear thought Ohio was the Promised Land, now you up here saying the same thang!"

Cleve's merriment softened Elaine's disposition.

"C'mon, let's make it."

As they rose to leave, Cleve left a few quarters behind on their table.

THEY HADN'T MADE IT A MILE NORTH ON TELEGRAPH before a squad car pulled behind them.

"Oh shit." Cleve muttered.

Elaine gathered her rocks in her lap.

What was really less than a minute was extended by the foreboding silence.

"BOY, DON'T YOU KNOW AIN'T NO NEGROES 'ROUND THIS neighborhood. Step out the car."

"We ain't stepping outta shit!" Elaine screamed.

The officer nodded his head to his partner which conveyed to the partner to go and call for back up.

Cleve's teeth clenched. He took slow breaths and closed his eyes.

"Get out the gotdam car now you coon!"

When Cleve opened the door, the officer had already drawn his pistol. He aimed it at Cleve's temple as he rose from the car.

"OH HELL NAWL!" Elaine roared as she jumped out the passenger door.

Cleve didn't even know her name to warn her to be cool.

Before he could place the call, the other cop dropped the

mic, and raced from squad car as Elaine launched a rock over the roof.

The pistol-wielding officer ducked and let off a shot in the air.

His partner tackled Elaine.

Cleve fell away from the fired shot, attempted to get up and over to the other side of the car.

"Freeze or the next bullet will be in your ass!"

Cleve stood with his hands up.

On the other side of car, Elaine kicked, tussled and otherwise made it impossible for the officer to subdue her. All while screaming, "Death to the pigs! Death to the pigs!"

"Calling all cars! Calling all cars!" blared from the police speakers. The officer with the gun fired another shot to get Elaine's attention. She froze and his partner scrambled to his feet as if recovering from a bout with the Tasmanian Devil. Both officers backed away and headed to their car.

The gun-toter warned, "Get your asses out of here before we arrest you!" They slammed their doors, squealed the tires into a u-turn, and blasted their sirens as they pulled away.

Elaine screamed, "Bitches!!!" as she hurled another rock.

SHE MISSED.

8

WHY CAN'T WE BE FRIENDS?

War

Monday, November 4, 2013

*H*is face was tomato red and streaked with tears. His sobs were sporadic and his words were muttered with a trembling that was suppose to convey sincerity.

Richard Gilliam was flanked by Armstrong Thomas and Reverend Amos Thigpen, whose hand rested upon Gilliam's shoulder.

With a performance worthy of an Oscar, Gilliam sobbed for the news cameras, "Detroit, I'm sorry. I'm sorry for my greed. I have been clinically diagnosed as bi-polar and that other side of me, that mental illness caused me to jeopardize my job and steal from your children."

Then Gilliam turned with a pained grief-stricken expression to Reverend Thigpen who patted him on the back while consoling, "Allow the Lord to use you. Tell the peoples it won't happen again."

Pitifully, Gilliam turned back to the television cameras

and boo-hoo'ed some more. "I'm just really sorry. I know you people have been through so much since slavery and then my other half did stupid things with the money that was meant for your kids." He then pounded the palm of his hand against his forehead three times.

A father who was dropping off his children saw the charade from the hallway outside the library. When Gilliam paused, the father shouted, "Just give us back the damn money and stop all that bullshit!"

In response, Reverend Thigpen bumped Gilliam aside, grabbed the microphone, and spoke with a such condescending force that his jowls shook. "We won't have none of that mister!" He then shot an evil glare from over the rim of his glasses, as he forced his chin down into his blubbery neck, and pursed his lips in a wide frown that stretched across his face.

He then gathered himself, looked directly into the television camera and said, "Last night, the Lord laid it on my heart to forgive our brother." He cast a pitying look over to the dry heaving Gilliam. "Because I serve a Gawd of MERCY! I serve a Gawd of grace. Wherefore our savior has challenged us all when he said unto the father, FATHER, forgive them ..." Thigpen did a survey of the room before driving home his point. "For they know not what they do."

Thigpen extended his arm around the shoulder of Gilliam and drew him close. "Brother Gilliam knew not what he did. DEEtroit I have seen the PAPERS saying this man," Thigpen lightly tapped Gilliam with his pointer finger. "This man right here, this servant of Gawd, this accountant for the well-being of the chillun', Detroit I seen the papers documenting his illness, his bi-polarism. But Gawd said to me, he said, AMOS!! Pray for that man. Make that man whole again. Show the peoples of Detroit what forgiveness looks like."

With that he turned to Richard Gilliam, caressed the sides of his face, and kissed him on the cheek.

"Brother Gilliam! You are forgiven." Reverend Thigpen pronounced as he dutifully shook Gilliam's hand as Armstrong Thomas stood in the background, smiling like a proud minstrel.

9

THE CLOSER I GET TO YOU

Roberta Flack & Donny Hathaway

Thursday July 27, 1967

*E*laine awakened first.

They had been holed up in a motor lodge not far from Buick City in Flint. Each night, Cleve slept on the floor while allowing Elaine to enjoy the comforts of the bed. Yesterday, he had awakened first, slipped away, and returned with some breakfast.

It was only day two; yet, Elaine had arose with the hope that he would repeat the breakfast routine. That hope was a reflection of her longing for a life of consistency.

She leaned over the edge of the bed. There he lay between the door and the bed like some type of bodyguard.

She took a moment to reflect on him, how they met, the time they have been spending together, and how he wasn't trying to have sex with her. Until she met Cleve, she was sure all men just wanted to have sex as soon as possible. Nothing is wrong with sex, but can people at least learn each other's names first?

She chuckled a little, remembering he didn't learn her

name until they had just about arrived at the hotel. After the episode with the police, they rode in silence for an hour until she asked, "Where are you taking me?"

Apparently, his thoughts had taken him beyond the car.

"Wait, hunh?" he replied.

"Cleveland, where are we going? Where are you taking me?"

"Um um, you know, what? I don't even know your name. What's your name?"

"Elaine. Now... where are we going?"

"When I left my pad earlier, I was intending on going to Flint. You know, thinking that might be far enough from the action."

"Flint? You made plans to go to Flint?" Elaine quipped sarcastically.

"Hold on now," Cleve paused to recall her name, "Elaine. You ever been to Flint?"

She shook her head, "No."

"So how you gonna talk bad about it? Look, I got some peoples up there and when I'm there, shoot, it's good times all around!"

"Your girlfriend lives there? Cleveland, are you taking a lady stranger to your girlfriend's house?"

If facial expressions could be interpreted to language, Cleve's expression would have said, "What in the hell are you talking about?"

Elaine read his expression correctly and added, "I don't want to be a part of your revelry. Just take me back to Detroit."

"Revelry? What in the world?" Cleve was getting irritated. "Take you back to Detroit? That's what you want? So you and your damn rocks can get rolled over by a tank? Yeah, that's a great idea!"

Elaine folded her arms in a huff and her nostrils flared so wide they doubled their size.

Cleve continued, "Look I'm all about fighting for my rights and shit. But gotdamn girl, I mean, Elaine, what the hell them rocks gonna do?"

She heard him but rolled her eyes in defiance.

"Check this out, you get a better plan for sticking it to the man and I promise I'll help you get that thing going. But Elaine, you gonna have to have something way more solid than throwing rocks."

A few moments of silence passed before Cleve restated, more softly and assuringly, "I promise."

Elaine looked at him and relaxed her nostrils.

WHEN THEY CHECKED IN THE MOTOR LODGE ON TUESDAY night, Cleve announced, "I packed enough clothes for a couple of days. You can have one of my shirts for a nightgown if you don't want to sleep in your clothes." He placed his bag on the bed. "I'm going to go down to machine and grab a pop or something, you want anything?"

"No, I'm okay," was her response but she was looking at Cleve in disbelief. She didn't really have a home back in Detroit and the people she stayed with probably assumed she was staying somewhere else. She wasn't accustomed to any one, especially a man, caring for her in the way Cleveland was. Although she thought it was a stupid question, just for assurance she asked, "Are you coming back?"

Cleve froze as he stood in the doorway. He heard her but it seemed like she was asking something more than whether he was returning from the vending machine. He nodded his head slowly, "Yeah, I'm coming back ... I ... I didn't bring you up here to leave you."

Elaine smiled at him for the first time.

. . .

SHE WAS ALSO SMILING AS SHE WATCHED HIM SLEEPING ON the floor. Really, she should have been alarmed. She's in a strange place, in a strange city, with a strange man. But if actions speak louder than words, then Cleveland's actions said he is going to take care of her. His actions said that he was going to protect her. While she knew she could protect herself, she felt comforted by his actions and intent.

She reached to gently push his shoulder. As he stirred, she warmly said, "Good morning, Cleveland."

When he turned toward her voice and opened his eyes, he saw the smile that would warm many of his future days.

10

IF THERE'S HELL BELOW, WE'RE ALL GONNA GO

Curtis Mayfield

Tuesday, November 5, 2013

*S*usan Van Vetchen banged the gavel and called to order a special meeting of the Ella Baker Academy School Board. Van Vetchen was the board chair and the heiress of Van Vetchen estate. A well-connected liberal socialite, she often donated her time and money to causes of public service. Womanists around the city viewed her contributions with a disbelieving side-eye as they recognized that Van Vetchen's gifts were only given to matters to which she became the voice, the public face, and controller of the agenda.

Reverend Amos Thigpen was viewed by some as Van Vetchen's personal lap dog. If anyone spoke unflatteringly about Van Vetchen, he would unleash a vitriolic attack about their intent and how his god knows no color, just good will.

The other members of the Ella Baker School Board were Armstrong Thomas, Abdul Sharif, and Melba McLeod. Sharif was a self-proclaimed Black Nationalist, who nearly always offered valuable insight, thoughtful projections, and rich historical context. However, his intelligence was undermined by his ironclad patriarchy and homophobia. Typically, when he prefaced his stance with "Unapologetically African" it was an attempt to cover the shortcomings of his position. All board debates ended with Sharif on the far left and Thomas on the far right.

McLeod was the board vote tie-breaker. A widowed single-mother whose husband had who mysteriously died in police custody, McLeod was nearing the end of her law school studies. She was the conscious of the group and the board member who spent the most time talking with parents and visiting classrooms. Her son was a fifth grader at Ella Baker.

"I HEREBY CALL TO ORDER THIS SPECIAL BOARD MEETING for the Ella Baker Academy. As everyone should know, our school has come under a bit of scrutiny due to the financial shenanigans of ..."

Attorney Mankiller bolted upright, "I object!"

Glances were passed around the audience. Everyone figured this would be a fight and it appeared punches were going to be thrown from the opening bell.

Van Vetchen was bothered and the growing redness in her face conveyed that idea. She looked around at the other board members while mumbling into the microphone, "Well, I never ..."

Mankiller pounced, "Mrs. Van Vetchen, we are not here to debate what you have never experienced in your privileged life. We are here to publicly present the truth about Principal Robeson's actions and intentions. Your 'financial shenanigans' statement was a premature indictment of Principal Robeson's actions. That statement is more fitting of the former CFO Richard Gilliam, who previously worked for the Van Vetchen

Foundation. However, these hearings are dedicated to Principal Robeson's truth."

Van Vetchen shot a quick glance to Reverend Thigpen, who snatched the microphone from the front of her and bellowed, "We will have order Attorney Mankiller! Order. It is the Lord's way!" He then clasped the lapels of his suit jacket as if to convey, 'I'm in charge here.'

Mankiller was unfazed. The pursing of her lips and sidewards tilting of her head preceded her response, "Is this the same Lord that led you to forgive Mr. Gilliam or some other Lord of your choosing?"

Van Vetchen pounded the gavel several times. "Order. Order. Order."

Attorney Mankiller took her seat next to Elaine Robeson.

An exasperated Van Vetchen started again, "I hereby call to order this special board meeting." She cut her eyes in Mankiller's direction as she proceeded, "To address the charges made against Principal Elaine Robeson." Mankiller returned a faint smirk of satisfaction.

THE AGENDA WAS SET IN ADVANCE AND DESIGNED TO encompass several board meetings. Van Vetchen had proposed only presentations related to the charges. Sharif advocated for parents, students, and other community members to speak. Thomas vacillated between both sides. Thigpen abstained from suggestions because he proclaimed that the board chairperson's suggestions incorporated his own ideas. McLeod deliberated the longest. She emphasized that while the meetings were not legal proceedings, they would take on the appearance of trial. It was as if she was weighing the pros and cons of Van Vetchen and Sharif's suggestions. Yet, the longer she talked, the more her ideas aligned with the wisdom of Sharif's promotion of hearing from those served. She recommended that it only seemed fair that the board hear both sides if they were seeking the truth. Moreover, she projected that the public attention paid to the case would impact enrollment and that the choice to ignore the voice of the people would lead to decline in enrollment. She swayed Thomas with her reasoning and the agenda proposed by Sharif became the template for the meetings to follow. By the end of their closed session, Van Vetchen attempted to convey that such an agenda had been her idea all along. Thigpen endorsed her unsubstantiated attempt by describing her preliminary position as that of playing the devil's advocate. The session concluded with Sharif mocking Thigpen by saying, "The Devil got enough advocates as it is Rev. Let's be clear about whether or not you're one of 'em."

NATURAL WOMAN

Aretha Franklin

Thursday July 27, 1967

*E*ternity passed as Cleve laid on his back looking into Elaine's smile. Almost as if her eyes had become crystal balls forecasting their future together. Slowly, he reached up and his fingertips met her left cheek. Elaine leaned into his palm as his fingers slowly cupped behind her ear and entered her afro just above her neck.

Elaine closed her eyes for a moment. Her bliss was slowly being overtaken by bashfulness. As bashfulness began to gain an advantage, she squeezed her eyelids tight to avoid opening them and finding that her heart was lying. Recognizing her conflict, Cleve leaned up and planted a soft, lingering kiss in the middle of her forehead. The kiss melted away Elaine's bashfulness.

Then Cleve rose to his knees and placed his other hand on the side of Elaine's face. Her normal defensiveness oozed away between his fingers leaving her nervous and vulnerable. Cleve placed a gentle kiss on the tip of her nose and she giggled softly. Very slowly, Elaine opened her eyes and met

Cleve's. With promises communicating between their gazes, Cleve took one hand and his fingertips delicately followed the arch of her eyebrow, over her temple, up and around her ear, down her neck, and then he extended his finger under her chin. When he leaned forward, Elaine closed her eyes for a kiss. But he didn't kiss. The tip of his nose met hers and his lips rested upon her lips. He didn't kiss, he just sort of rested there. When Elaine opened her eyes, Cleve was there, patient and gentle.

Elaine initiated a very hungry kiss as she stepped off the mattress and pushed Cleve back to the floor. When his head rested upon the pillow he had been using, she sat straddling his waist. Her hands pressed against his shoulders and she studied his eyes. Then with her hands, she made a large Y across his torso until the tips of both her middle fingers nestled into his belly button. He brought his palms to rest atop her thighs.

"I've never been in love before," said one.

After nearly a minute of silence, "Neither have I," said the other.

Elaine reversed the "Y" she made with hands from his belly button, along the center of his stomach, across his chest, and with gentle nudging at his armpits, encouraged him to splay his arms and hands upward. With that, her hands smoothly glided along the inside of his upper arm, over the elbow crooks, and forearm. Once at his palms, her fingers spread into an intertwine with his.

In a pose that a seasoned yogi would admire, she didn't bring her body to rest atop his. Instead, she hovered, with only her nipples reaching out for contact. Cleve relaxed and followed her lead.

With a soft head nudge from Elaine, Cleve lifted his chin and she leaned down to kiss him on his collar. Her kiss lingered without force or haste. She then kissed him on his

Adam's Apple. She kissed under his jaw. His chin. His lips. His nose. Then she did a mild retreat where the bridge of her nose came to rest along the curve of his neck. Her body relaxed on top of his as she squeezed his hands tightly.

Cleve whispered, "You know 'Laine. This thing. Once we do this. It ain't no turning back."

Elaine leaned close and replied, "Don't give me a reason to turn back and I won't."

12

WHO'S GONNA TAKE THE WEIGHT?

Kool & the Gang

Tuesday, November 12, 2013

*T*he first witness called by the school board was Thaddeus James.

Mr. James was the father of a first grader, A'Lexxus. Often assumed to be her grandfather, sixty-year old Thaddeus had spent most of his adult life as a player, philanderer, and sponsor of shopping excursions. He fancied himself a pimp and was known to spout Iceberg Slim inspired couplets although there weren't any women foolish enough to turn their earnings over to him. He was more of a delusional sugar daddy who told the younger women that he preyed upon to call him "the Messiah," because his game was so strong. Apparently, the player got played by a woman whose baby-in-a-basket-on-the-doorstep strategy brought an end to Thaddeus' womanizing ways.

One look at A'Lexxus' wide nose and densely thick eyebrows and there was no mistaking that Thaddeus was the father. Moreover, the charm he used to manufacture to deceive women effused naturally from his daughter. If ever there was a time to retire his player card, it was when he accepted the mantle of single parenthood. A mantle he mishandled despite his good intentions.

Once when A'Lexxus was a kindergartener, Principal Robeson personally walked her to Thaddeus' Cadillac Escalade during dismissal. The James family consisted of only Thaddeus and A'Lexxus, but the oversized SUV with designer rims and tires matched Mr. James' outsized ego.

"What's crackin' Mrs. Robeson?" Thaddeus shouted as the passenger window lowered.

"Mr. James, did you know that A'Lexxus is five? Elaine asked dryly.

"Oh hell yeah, I knew that! That's my baby girl! What's it to you?" he replied before holding up one finger to Principal Robeson and then shouting into his bluetooth earpiece, "Yeah, yeah, Chuck? Man, I gotta holla back atcha later. Lexxus' principal is here." A short pause, then he shouted, "Alright champ, don't take no wooden nickels!" He was still laughing his 'heh-heh-heh' chuckle when he unlocked the door. Elaine opened the door so that A'Lexxus could hop-in.

"Mr. James, I thought it was a little much when I realized that your daughter is the only kindergartener who frequents the hair salon; but considering your circumstances, I understood."

She continued, "I found it to be a bit of overkill when I was made aware that A'Lexxus has a different pair of Jordans for each day of the week."

Thaddeus inserted, "Aww Principal Robeson, you know how we treat baby girls. Why have 'em if ya ain't gonna spoil them? Heh-heh-heh."

Elaine was not persuaded. She resumed, "Mr. James, I am going to ask you two things. First, please do not send A'Lexxus to school with this mink jacket anymore. Second, why don't you join us on Saturday? You might hear some good ideas from the other parents."

"Principal Robeson, I can't promise that. I gotta keep my baby warm! Heh-heh-heh."

"Yes, but..." recognizing that he would not see her logic, she tried a different approach. "You know the kindergarteners hang their things on the hooks outside their classroom. I would hate for something to happen to her jacket, you get what I'm saying?"

Thaddeus pondered it a moment then asked, "The little peoples is thieving now? Shit, they jacking crayons and er'thang nowadays!"

Elaine crossed her fingers and took a deep breath. Thaddeus resumed, "Bet. I 'preciate the heads up. Lex ain't gonna where the mink no mo'. Shit, something happen to my baby's coat I might have stab one these fools."

"What about Saturday?" Elaine inquired.

"I thought that shit was for the po' parents. We good Mrs. Robeson, we got plenty to eat."

"Oh no Mr. James, our Saturday sessions aren't just about food. It's a time for parents to support each other. Especially single parents like yourself. You could learn simple things like how braid A'Lexxus' hair or which pediatricians are the best. You don't have to be poor to participate."

Thaddeus raised an eyebrow in contemplation, rubbed his knuckle under his daughter's chin causing her to smile, and then looked back at Principal Robeson. "Alright, since you insist. We'll see you on Saturday."

———

THE PROCEEDINGS BEGAN WITH BOARD CHAIR VAN Vetchen's questions.

"Please state your name for the record."

"My name is Thaddeus James."

"What is your relationship with the Ella Baker Academy?"

"My baby girl, A'Lexxus James, is a first grader there and er'y now and then, I do a little somethin' with the PTA."

"Have you ever participated in the Saturday Sessions at Ella Baker?"

"You mean, the thing where they give the po' kids breakfast and the parents have like a little meeting thing going on?"

"If that is how you describe it; yes, that is what we mean by the Saturday Sessions."

"Yeah, I done been several times. Might even be whatcha call a regular, know what I mean? Heh-heh-heh." No one else laughed, so he continued. "Yeah, so like I say, I done been a couple times. Now before ya ask, I started last year when 'Lexxus was in the kiddie garden. Mrs. Robeson axed me to come, and so hey! I was like, 'we'll be there.'"

"Mr. James, describe what happens during the Saturday Sessions."

"So yeah, like I say, we or er'ybody thats coming that day meet up at the school er'y Saturday at nine in the morning. Then usually Mrs. Robeson, she already be there you know. Mrs. Robeson and about four of the teachers opens the doors for us to come in. Then they split us up. The chil'ren, they follows the teachers down to the cafeteria where they eat first and do some tutoring stuff. The parents? We go with Mrs. Robeson to the library where she got the chairs in a circle like. Heh-heh-heh." His laugh proceeded what he though was a joke. "I mean that circle put me in the mind of AA meetings. You know Alcoholics Anonymous? Yeah, when I was a young buck the judge said it was either that or a couple of months in the county jail - so you know, hey! Send me to the meetings. Heh-heh-heh."

Van Vetchen shared a diplomatic smirk before asking Mr.

James to continue his description. She also inquired about the number of participants.

Looking to sky and scratching his chin, Mr. James responded, "Its always way mo' kids than parents. I think most of dem kids just walk over from the projects. They parents ain't stuting nothin' 'bout whatcha call 'Saturday Sessions.' Nawl, they just send dem kids over unsupervised and er'ything. But it ain't neva no problems or nuthin' 'cause dem kids know Mrs. Robeson don't play!! Heh-heh-heh."

Again, no one laughed.

"Yeah so um, I'd say it be like twenty, thirty kids and 'bout ..." Those paying attention could see Mr. James reflectively count the parents in his mind. "Um, bout seven parents, maybe fifteen onna really good day. But yeah, you can count on at least seven. Seven fa' sho going to be there."

"What do the parents do in the library?"

"At first, I was like, 'I ain't got time fa' dis.' But then what be happenin' is we talk about stuff parent-to-parent like. I tell ya' it feels like AA though cause Mrs. Robeson, she like the sponsor or whatever, she kinda put a question out there, a couple of folks might say a little something, then BOOM! Its like she axe that question again, harder though. Man shoot, some of da times the little mamas be cryin' and carrying on like confessionals. Then Mrs. Robeson'll give a hug and stuff then give some good answers to the questions she axed!"

"Can you provide us with an example?"

"Oh yeah. Like one of da times, I think it was my first time, but yeah, Mrs. Robeson started talkin' 'bout what she call 'proper nutrition and diet.' I was like, 'Mrs. Robeson, I ain't trying to lose no weight!' Heh-heh-heh, but the little mamas just kinda rolled they eyes at me and whatnot so I just kinda kept to myself, you know what I mean. But Mrs. Robeson went in about sugary foods and Flamin' Hot Cheetos. Let me tell ya'll, you wanna get Mrs. Robeson mad, bring some of dem Flamin' Hot Cheetos - boy, she gonna start trippin'!! Heh-heh-heh."

That garnered a few chuckles from the audience and encouraged James to continue.

"But anyway that whole conversation turned into why we should get fresh fruit from the Eastern Market rather than buying gummy bears and what not. You know, I hadn't thought about it before but what I did for the next week is I bought a whole bushel of the reddest strawberries to the meeting so the little mamas could take some when they leave."

"Were all of the meetings conducted in this manner?"

"You mean, Mrs. Robeson giving us life tips and whatnot? Yeah, kinda. Some of the times one of the parents would have a really good idea. Like one of the little mamas, she was a regular too, she was talkin' 'bout this doctor who told her that the ADHD label on her kid was wrong. Maaaan, I think all the parents in the meetings started going to that doctor after that! Heh-heh-heh."

A few "Amens" came from the audience.

"Yep, just about all the meetings went that way. And then boom! At noon? We was outta there."

Van Vetchen looked to Attorney Mankiller and then her fellow board members, "Are there any additional questions for Mr. James?"

All of the heads nodded 'no'.

"Thank you Mr. James."

"Aww no problem. It's easy talkin' 'bout Mrs. Robeson. She da truth."

13

SO GOOD TO BE HOME WITH YOU

Tyrone Davis

Tuesday, November 12, 2013

"*H*ow did it go?" asked Tanya as Stokely made his way to the living room.

Whenever they had a long day, Stokely and Tanya developed a sort of intimate debriefing practice on their sofa. Tanya, who had arrived home earlier, was already in her pajamas seated on the sofa with her back on the arm rest. As a design engineer, Tanya had a collection of sketch pads around their apartment and this unwinding time on the sofa usually including her doodling designs in one of her pads.

After removing his coat, Stokely continued to undress until he was down to a t-shirt and his boxers. Then standing behind Tanya, he sank his hands into her dreadlocks until his fingers reached her skin. Then he cradled her head, tilted it upward, leaned over and kissed her forehead and her nose. This kissing pattern instantly transformed Tanya from artist-executive to blushing school girl.

Stokely made his way to the other end of the sofa. Once

seated, he turned so that his back would be against the armrest opposite of Tanya. Within seconds, Tanya would slowly extend one of her long legs into Stokely's lap. Considering her six foot height, the length of her legs was a delightful study in musculature. Stokely caught her foot and held it with both hands. He began with his thumbs pressed together and he would slowly work them upward from her heel to her toes. Then he would separate his thumbs to work the outer edges of her sole before paying attention to each toe. First, he would bend the toe, straighten it, and then tug slightly as if aligning.

To her inquiry, Stokely sighed before answering.

"It's pretty obvious some of the board members have it out for my mom." He paused while thinking of what to say next. His thumbs were pressing tightly and making small circles in her sole.

"It's like they would ask these one-sided questions, loaded questions - you know the kind lawyers use to trick people?"

Tanya's "Mmm-hmmmm" was in response to the question and the foot massage.

"They would try that shit but then the person on the stand would answer in a way that made my mom look even more heroic than she would have ever described her own work."

Tanya placed her other foot in his lap as he continued.

"Two of the board members kept comparing her to the finance guy who admitted to stealing money. They talked like my mom was in cahoots with him. Like they planned a criminal enterprise or something. But if you compare their actions, you know, what each of them did with the money - it's a whole different story."

Tanya knew the longer he talked, the longer she would enjoy the massage, so she continued to ask questions.

"Did Elaine explain the difference on the witness stand?"

"Nah, she didn't take the stand tonight. Tonight was just like protocol review, then a long soliloquy by the shady preacher dude, and one testimony from one of the dads who participated in the weekend program my mom set-up."

"So exactly how were they comparing her to the guilty guy?"

"That's what's so crazy, the preacher dude was trying to evoke Jesus and whatnot." Then Stokely began to laugh. "Tanya, baby, dude tried to compare his stance against my mother to Jesus turning over tables in the temple."

Tanya erupted in laughter while managing to say, "That is ridiculous!"

"He is ridiculous. The other board members were ... well, it's five of them. Preacher dude had the most to say. The board chair is a rich white lady, who not only seemed out of place, but also seems to use the preacher as a house negro."

Tanya flinched at the description and the tender spot Stokely worked on her foot.

Stokely changed his massage pattern. He bent her foot down as far it could go and held it for several seconds. Then he bent it back and held it there. He followed this by intertwining his fingers with her toes and rotating her foot in a circular motion for several turns one way then the other.

"There is also like this super pro-black dude, a real conservative cat, then a professional lady. Actually, I think they will be voices of reason because Reverend what's-his-face and Missy surely have their own agenda."

"How was your mother during the testimony?"

"Honestly, she is still in a state of shock. Little emotion. Damn near stoic. Leaning on my dad almost like a blind person with a guide." Stokely switched his flexing routine to the other foot. "I'm guessing she never imagined she would be made into a public pariah. But really, is she a pariah or is this whole situation being sensationalized for someone else's benefit?"

Tanya replied, "I think that's it exactly."

14

I'LL TAKE YOU THERE

The Staple Singers

August 1967

"Can I ask you a question?" Elaine inquired as they proceeded southward on Interstate 75.

They had been nearly inseparable since the days following the rebellion and true to his word, Cleve was helping her start her freshmen year at Wilberforce.

"Yeah," Cleve responded while preparing for the worst.

"I don't know any factory guys that would help their girlfriends go to school. Especially away to school."

Cleve added a "Mmm-hmmm."

A silence loomed for the moments before Elaine breached her fears. Her experiences with Cleve had been consistent and proven that what she thought she knew about men very seldom applied to Cleve. Her experiences did not eliminate her fears but did provide a bit of courage to ask at least some of the questions that came to mind.

"When you drop me off, are we done?"

Cleve damn near swerved off the road.

Tuesday, November 12, 2013

"I'M DONE," SAID ELAINE.

Cleve was not sure he heard correctly so he slowed to the side of Jefferson Ave. while allowing an ambulance with blaring sirens to speed around him and zoom through the intersection.

Elaine's silence had been worrying him and the randomness of her proclamation exacerbated that worry.

After more than forty years of marriage, Cleve could only recall a handful of times when his wife retreated into this type of stoic quietness. The first time was when he accompanied her to Arkansas to meet her parents. The visit with her mother would have otherwise been bad except that the meeting with her father was so dreadful that the impersonal disconnection with her mother was the lesser of the evils. When Elaine's father looked through her as if she were a stranger, Elaine was rattled. Considering the stories she shared, Cleve knew that they had never met; however, the "What-can-I-do-for-you" casualness he extended when they did meet confirmed her anonymity to him and darkened her hopes.

But this silence seemed to surpass that heartbreak in destitution.

"'Laine ... you feel like walking?"

"Yeah ..." she replied as if she would say more, but she didn't.

Cleve parked in front of the Coleman A. Young Municipal Center. Before he reached the other side she was out of the car. She slammed the door and shouted, "What did I do to deserve this?!"

Cleve paused. He reached tentatively for her hand like someone attempting to defuse a bomb. She clasped it while continuing her vent. "I did not take any money! Everybody knows that! Not a cent. Zilch. Nada. Nothing!"

Cleve tugged her so that she would follow him across the street to Hart Plaza and the Riverwalk.

Whenever they faced problems that required discussion, they took it to the water. Or more specifically, they walked along various parts of the Detroit River. It seemed that the current of water facilitated a current of emotion from Elaine. Cleve first noticed the parallels in the 1970s and stuck with the strategy ever since.

It wasn't as cold as it could be in Detroit during November. Plus the fire in Elaine's spirit would thaw out the most severe of ice storms.

Hart Plaza was empty save for a homeless person pushing a cart of his belongings. When the homeless guy saw them, he was going to approach. But Cleve's stern glare and head nod, no, communicated to the homeless man to continue on his way.

Elaine was on a roll and never saw the homeless person.

"That is why I left DPS. Way too many people in power pocketing money and me, someone who is trying to do right - the press attacks me! I mean DAMN did they need a new Kwame Kilpatrick to demonize? C'mon Cleveland, you're a rationale man, tell it to me straight. I'mma big girl, I can take it. Why me?!"

While rhetorical in nature, Elaine's question caused Cleve to stop. They had neared the Riverwalk and were just in front of the Underground Railroad statue. Cleve took a deep breath and reached for Elaine's other hand.

"You know 'Laine, I ain't one them conspiracy theorists. But I ..."

A flash of anger crossed his face before he continued. "I think this whole thing against you. I think it is keeping us from seeing what's really going on."

This time Elaine tugged him to continue their walk. They proceeded toward the Renaissance Center.

"This Gilliam cat cleared over a million before his dirt was exposed. But the thing that gets me is why it was exposed now. It ain't like y'all was undergoing an audit or nothing."

Cleve's inquiry segued Elaine from venting anger to contemplative dialogue. She responded, "When you put it that way, it makes me think back to those last couple of years when I was with DPS."

Cleve nodded in agreement because he had a feeling where his wife was headed.

"All that newspaper talk about how bad Detroit Public Schools was conveniently excluded the financial stability of the district. Then ..." Elaine's voice trailed off from the lingering disappointment of the memory.

"Then the state took over. Five years later, DPS was in the red."

She looked at Cleve, who already knew the story but was listening along.

"Before the state takeover, DPS had a surplus. Since the state takeover, DPS has been in a deficit every year."

Cleve added, "And most of us didn't see it until it was over."

Wistfully, Elaine continued. "We didn't. We didn't see it. I mean, it never felt right. Like since when did Lansing give a damn about Detroit kids? But we didn't see it ..."

Regretfully, Cleve chimed in, "Until it was too late."

They continued walking in silence with Elaine squeezing Cleve's hand tightly. They were attempting to see past their anger, trying to gain some focus of the real intent and the real manipulators of the distracting spectacle against Elaine.

August 1967

"WE ARE NOT DONE," CLEVE REPLIED AFTER PARKING THE car on the highway shoulder.

He restated for added emphasis, "No, we are not done."

His stare at her was not intended to be intimidating. His stare was intended to convey his sincerity.

He pointed to himself. "I'm going to get you to school."

He pointed to her. "You are going to graduate."

His finger went back and forth between them. "We are just getting started."

His certainty silenced Elaine's worries and warmed her heart.

15

NO ONE IN THE WORLD

Anita Baker

Tuesday, November 19, 2013

The second witness called by the school board was Matthesia Phillips.

Mrs. Phillips was the mother of a fourth grader, Deonte. Her appearance on the stand matched her everyday disposition - that of a woman stressed, hurried, and barely making it. Mrs. Phillips' husband served in Afghanistan and only looks like the man she married prior to his deployment. The emotional trauma he experienced during military service rendered him a shell of a man with extreme mood swings and frequent episodes of disappearing from home. Mrs. Phillips is carrying the weight of his plummeting psyche and fractures within their home on her body and in her soul. His veteran benefits were not enough to match their family expenses nor did they fully cover the significant psychiatric care he needs. Moreover, Deonte is old enough to make some sense of his father's problems and this awareness troubles him in ways he cannot articulate.

· · ·

Van Vetchen began, "Please state your name for the record."

Mrs. Phillips responded, "My name is Matthesia Phillips. My friends call me Mattie but you all should call me Mrs. Phillips." The statement was a precursor to Mrs. Phillips position on matters.

Reverend Thigpen interjected, "Sister Phillips, what is your relationship with Ella Baker Academy?"

She corrected him in her reply. "Call me, Mrs. Phillips," then she waited.

Reverend begrudgingly relented, "Mrs. Phillips."

Mattie smirked before she responded, "I learned about Ella Baker when I was member of your church. Once I enrolled my son, Deonte, I stayed with the school even after I left your church."

Mrs. McLeod asked, "How long has your son been an Ella Baker student?"

"He started in kindergarten and he is in fourth grade now."

McLeod then inquired, "Please explain your relationship with Principal Robeson."

Mattie took a deep breath, chuckled, and then began, "Back when I was at Pastor Thigpen's church, he told me about this new school he was working with. At that time, he was dissing the principal - Principal Robeson, that is." Mrs. Phillips appeared steady in her recollection of what he said, "We got one those DPS rejects but just work with us and we'll get an anointed leader in there soon enough."

Thigpen cleared his throat and straightened his tie.

Mattie rolled her eyes and continued, "But once I got to the school, everything and everyone felt like family. I met Principal Robeson during the kindergarten registration and she was helpful and knowledgable. You know now that I think about it, she was working the door and escorting families to the appropriate stations. I never seen a school leader all helpful like that."

Sharif jumped in, "Can you say more about what you mean when you say 'never seen a school leader work like that'?"

Phillips acquiesced. "Yeah, sure." For a moment, her eyes wandered as the film reel of memories dialed back to an early interaction with Principal Robeson. "You know, I can tell you exactly when I really met Principal Robeson. Deonte was in first grade and my husband didn't pick him up from school. It was the last day before Christmas break and I'm sure Principal Robeson was ready to go home like everyone else. We didn't have a phone but at 5:15, I answered the door and there was Principal Robeson and Deonte. I was embarrassed, scared, angry, and a bunch of other stuff."

Some board members and a number of people in the audience leaned forward as it appeared that Mattie Phillips was no longer at the forum but instead, fully transported into her memories. She continued, "Deonte was talking a mile a minute as he started to cry. That was the first time Rick was suppose to pick him up and didn't show. I had spent the day moving into our smaller apartment and just, just ..."

Tears began to flow. Board member Armstrong Thomas left his seat and took a box of Kleenex to where Mrs. Phillips was.

She grabbed several and mouthed a "Thank-you" before attempting to proceed.

"Do you know how scary it is to watch your husband crumble, your son sees it, and it ain't a damn thing you can do about it?" The question was rhetorical but the helplessness it conveyed caused the hearts of everyone listening to drop a little.

"So there I was trying to pull Deonte close so that he'd stop rambling and then Principal Robeson wrapped her arms around me like my grandmama or somebody..." Mrs. Phillips' tears intensified. "I needed that hug." She began to sob. "I needed someone to understand and not judge me."

Those paying attention saw Mrs. Phillips' sobbing face turn into a harden sneer.

"You know that next day, I went to our pastor ..." her words trailed off as she pointed an accusatory finger toward Reverend Thigpen. "The pastor told me, if I was a more loving wife, lost a little weight, and made our home a love nest, then Rick would come home." The incredulity that accompanied her sneer was as potent on the stand as it was when Thigpen first spoke the words. She continued, "Here I am busting my ass to keep our home, our marriage together and somebody gonna blame me about losing some damn weight? I mean fuck them ..."

Thigpen lowered the gavel.

Phillips didn't stop. "...Fuck you."

Van Vetchen slapped her palm on the table but Phillips was a steamroller. "All this shit about Principal Robeson and all she ever did was help the kids and families and teachers and everybody and your ass ..." Phillips bolted up out of her chair. "You still blaming people and sprinkling Jesus all over your shit to make it smell good!"

Sharif inserted with a balance of support and firmness, "Sister. Mrs. Phillips, Mrs. Phillips..."

When her glare turned to him, he placed his palms together as if praying, nodded his head slowly, and added, "Mrs. Phillips, please."

Mattie looked to McLeod, then to Mankiller, and then to Robeson who was wrought with sadness. Mattie's chest was heaving in anger. Mankiller asked a question out of turn but no one objected.

"Did you ever attend a Saturday Session?"

Mrs. Phillips sat slowly, wiped her face, and took a deep breath. "Yes."

Mankiller asked softly, "Tell us about your experience."

Mattie's tone shifted. "We don't have a computer. So on Saturday, that's the only time Deonte can get on the internet. I mean unless I take him to the library but that's not often. But the teachers that's there on Saturday, they let him use the computer as they are doing their tutoring thing." She chuckled a bit. "Deonte, he likes Saturdays better than regular school."

Mankiller returned the smile before asking, "Did you participate too?"

With a final wipe of her eyes, Mattie nodded 'yes' while saying, "At first, I just kinda sat in the back, you know just seeing what it was all about and what not." Having gathered herself, she went on confidently, "Principal Robeson keeps it one hundred. I mean she don't come out of that mean social worker bag about failing our kids. Nawl, it's like she knows what we up against and kinda be like, 'here is some stuff to help.'"

Mattie smiled. "We was moving a lot, too much. And well … so like then, I was really using payday loans and stuff. One Saturday, Principal Robeson talked about budgeting. Like for real, she going there? But she did. Not only did she go there, she spotted me fifty dollars to open a credit union account. Like boom! Right there, well after that Saturday Session was over and I told her I didn't even have a bank account. She asked me how me and Deonte was going to get home. I said we was going to walk. Then she said, 'I'll give you a ride if you let me take you to the credit union.'"

Elaine smiled at the memory.

"Right there, that day, she took us to the credit union and I opened my first account. Principal Robeson old school, so she actually wrote out a check ..." A few laughs were heard in the audience. Mattie continued, "You know she never asked for the money back? But she was telling me about how this was better than payday loans." Mattie chuckled a little as she added, "It took me awhile after that but I ain't got no more of them paydays. In fact, I got fiddy right now to pay you back Mrs. Robeson."

Elaine cried.

Even Mankiller was moved but she managed to say, "I have no further questions."

16

STOP, LOOK, LISTEN (TO YOUR HEART)

The Stylistics

Thursday, November 21, 2013

*T*he tone was with man-to-man earnestness as Dr. Trotter told Cleve the truth.

"Cleve, brother we go way back. You been with me since I was getting started over at Herman Kieffer." Dr. Trotter placed a hand on Cleve's shoulder. "So I'm going to give it to you straight. You gotta do something about your blood pressure."

Cleve looked to Dr. Trotter and nodded knowingly.

In a moment, it was clear.

The people that others rely upon are referred to as 'the rock' - the steady force that keeps everything together. The wise know that even 'the rock' needs someone to lean on. Elaine has been the rock for a whole community and her rock rests upon Cleve's rock. While their marriage has been one of trading rock positions or one carrying the other during troublesome times; this season with the accusations against his wife placed fissures in Cleve's supportive rock.

"Cleve, you are sixty-six years old and you look great.

While I wish you weren't still doing the plumbing jobs at the rate you do, I also agree that your work keeps you going. But, right now, especially with what's going on with your wife, you got to make some changes unless you want us to start writing your obituary."

Dr. Trotter let his words permeate Cleve's thoughts. He could see Cleve's countenance slump a bit.

As a testament to their friendship, Trotter sat on his stool and said, "Run it down for me Cleve. Tell me what you're carrying and maybe I can make a few suggestions to lighten the load."

Cleve let an elongated sigh escape as his thoughts rewound back in time.

November 22, 1979

INITIALLY, ELAINE WAS VEHEMENTLY AGAINST TAKING their infant, Stokely, outside in the cold. But the 'Mommy please' barrage from their three-year old daughter, Songhai, and Cleve's steady assurance prompted her to begrudgingly go along to the annual Thanksgiving Parade in Downtown Detroit. After the parade's end, Cleve laid a sleeping Songhai across the backseat of their Cutlass Supreme and eyed the happiness on Elaine's face as she got comfortable in the front seat and loosened some of the bundles under which she had wrapped baby Stokely.

Cleve did not want to spoil the mood but waited until they were a few miles away before saying what was on his mind.

"You know 'Laine, don't look like it's gonna get no better. They're definitely going to close Dodge Main pretty soon."

A few seconds later, Elaine replied, "What does that do to your skilled trades apprenticeship?"

Cleve shook his head, "I don't know. The boys down at the local say I can still get the training to be a journeyman plumber even if Main closes. I'm not too sure but I'm going to see if I can find out on Monday."

Elaine looked over the seat to check on the sleeping Songhai.

"'Laine, I want you to think about what I'm about to say." Cleve paused both at the red light and in his speech. When the light turned green, he proceeded. "It ain't no mystery that them Japanese boys is kicking our ass every time they sell one of those little cars. And when I think of that, I ain't too sure if Dodge Main gonna be the last plant to close."

He looked over to see if she was following him. She was. He resumed, "So I'mma see bout this apprenticeship still being a thing after Main closes but I also got an idea for you, for us."

Elaine raised her head to him after checking on Stokely.

"What if you went down to Wayne State and got a masters degree and then moved out of the classroom?"

He paused before resuming. "Our money 'bout to be real tight, but the way I see it, you could get that jump in pay and be a principal or assistant principal by the time Song get to first grade."

Elaine followed Cleve's ideas to which she replied, "I hadn't thought about it but I can see where you're going." She hesitated, "But Cleve, that sounds like future planning. What about now or January, next year? What we going to do about the kids? How are we going to pay for me going to school?"

"Yeah. Well, I wanted to start the idea and see what you thought. Look, it's kinda shaky but you know, I can stay home with the kids while you teach. Then hopefully, you do the night classes and maybe some of the plumbing classes can be on the nights you ain't in school. Plus, this won't be the first time I busted my savings for you to go to school - I think it's an investment."

Elaine heard him. But she also didn't hear him. The thought of being a principal was so new to her and the imagining of it distracted her from the rest of Cleve's conversation. He continued to speak but Elaine was busy shaping a new image of herself.

November 21, 2013

"TROTTER, MAN, MY BABY GIRL BEING IN THE JOINT IS A muthafucka. We been fighting to get her free for years and I tell ya, fighting a fight that long put a shitload of doubt in a man's heart about whether he can win ..." Cleve's words trailed off in sadness.

Dr. Trotter attempted to keep him focused, "Okay, that's one, a big stressor, but it's one. Let's lay these stressors out on the table. Get them out in the open to see what we can do with them."

Cleve shifted to the present. "Speaking of fighting, I don't know how much fight Elaine got left. I'm thinking she might be broken behind this bullshit. It really feels like I'm holding her up. Ain't no thang 'cause I wouldn't have it no other way, know what I mean?"

Trotter nodded in agreement.

Cleve continued, "Yet this attorney. She's a beast on this case and in my wallet, man. But when you want the best, you gotta pay. So that's why I've been doing more plumbing work. Even got my son, Stokely, helping me more. You know more jobs for more money to pay these new expenses." Cleve was starting to focus. "So what is that Trotter, stressors two, three, and four?"

Trotter sort of laughed, "You mean there is more?"

Cleve said, "Sshheeeiittt Doc, it's a whole lotta more. Not only is Mankiller on Elaine's case, she is also doing some work to spring Song loose. I appreciate her work and believe it's going to make a big difference, so I can't be fucking around with the money. So there you go, more plumbing jobs." Cleve pounded his fist into an open palm. "Doc, I remember when I first was telling Elaine about doing plumbing as a skilled trade. I was like, 'long as people shitting and flushing toilets, folks gonna need a plumber.'" The memory made Cleve laugh. "Man, I thank God I kept applying to the skilled trades even after not making the cut five times. Plumbing gives me plenty opportunities to make some money. Shit, most times I have more jobs than I have time to do 'em." Cleve stroked his chin. "That's what's really helping me right now."

"Yeeeahhhh," Trotter inserted. "But we got to get you on a steady pace before your blood pressure goes up any further."

He paused for a moment.

"Cleve, don't laugh brother, but what if you and Elaine picked up a hobby?"

Cleve laughed, "A hobby? C'mon Doc, I'mma grown-ass man. I ain't got time for no hobby."

"Cleveland brother, I'm trying to keep your behind alive. Or I could prescribe some medicine that will kill your libido."

That got Cleve's attention, "You know a hobby don't sound half bad. Alright Trot, whatcha got?"

"Tomorrow night, you and Elaine go skating."

Cleve exploded in laughter. "Trot, man, what in the hell?"

Dr. Trotter pushed forward, "Nah, nah, Cleve, For real. It can be like a date night. But more importantly, it'll be good exercise and a stress reliever." He stood, placed his hand back on Cleve's shoulder, and used his other hand to point to Cleve's heart. "Most importantly, it'll be good for your heart."

Cleve got the point. He still chuckled a bit at the thought of skating as he asked, "Doc, where we going to do this at?"

"Northland. Where else?" Trotter replied and then continued, "But y'all got to go every Friday along with some other new fitness practices like maybe a one or two mile walk every day until your next check-up."

Cleve laughed heartily to avoid the fear of what high blood pressure could do to him. After laughing, he added, "Wait 'til I tell 'Laine this."

17

THAT'S WHAT FRIENDS ARE FOR

Dionne Warwick & Friends

Saturday, November 23, 2013

"So y'all really went skating last night, huh?" Stokely laughed as he removed the tools and pipes from the back of his truck.

"Dr. Trotter thought it would be a fun way for me to do something about my blood pressure but he didn't say shit about this soreness in my legs, gotdamn." Cleve leaned against the van and ran his hands up and down his thighs before continuing, "Look Stokely, you gonna have to take the lead today 'cause the ole boy is wore out from all that skating."

Stokely set the pipes on top of the new kitchen sink they were installing, then joked with his father, "You sure all y'all did was skate?"

Cleve cracked up, "Well Trotter did say it would be like a date night and you know I'm all about keeping the home fires burning."

They shared a laugh as they carried the materials into the house.

. . .

FRANCINE WAS HOLDING OPEN THE SIDE THE DOOR AS THEY approached. She and Joyce had already talked with Elaine about last night's skating adventure. Both Francine and Joyce were pleased to hear the laughter in their friend's voice. It was the first time in a couple of months that her voice wasn't mired in melancholy.

"Maybe you should stay back and rest Cleve. All that skating is for them young folks," Francine said only half-kidding.

"Aw, I got Stokely wit' me. We gonna knock this sink out in no time," Cleve replied.

Stokely placed the materials down and gave Francine a hug and a peck on the cheek. She asked, "When are you gonna settle down? You can't be chasing these women forever. Go on ahead and settle down and be a good daddy to some kids."

Stokely had become accustomed to these type of inquires. He did not pride himself as being what some could call a good catch - an employable man in his thirties with no claimed or unclaimed children. Nearly every woman who was beyond his dating age range cajoled him to settle down. More astutely though, Stokely recognized that Francine did not mention Tanya, his current girlfriend. One day he is going to ask his mother why did everyone get tight-lipped about Tanya lately. But that was a conversation for another day, right now he needed to answer his "auntie."

"Someday Aunt Francine, I'm going to get it all together," he said boyishly.

"That's what I mean, go on ahead and get it together before it's too late." With that she segued into Cleve and indirectly communicated to Stokely to get to work.

"Cleve, c'mon in here and tell me what done got into you? Whatever it is it got my sister gushing like a schoolgirl!"

Cleve should not have been surprised that Elaine had told her girlfriends about last night. In fact, he took it as confirmation that she had a good time and was not thinking about the bullshit with the school board.

Once they sat in the dining room, Cleve knew that not only was Stokely going to have to do the sink job alone but that his wife's friends needed his help. In the past, helping them meant helping her so he was game to do his part before Francine even asked.

"Elaine said y'all didn't fall but that y'all was skating so slow that everyone was whizzing past y'all!" Francine burst out laughing at the image of her friends slow-stepping around the skating rink.

Cleve carried the good-natured ribbing further, "Even as slow as we was skating, I'm still sore."

"Well, that means y'all gotta go more often!" This time, Francine's laugh segued into the real matter. "Cleve, Joyce and I gonna need your help."

Cleve simply nodded yes. Francine already knew he was willing, he just needed the details.

"Once Elaine left DPS, she hasn't been willing to step inside any Detroit Public School. All that haggling they gave her about retiring really pissed her off. So all that to say, she ain't coming to my school."

Cleve nodded again to show he was listening.

"But you know Joyce took over a charter school the same time that Elaine did."

Cleve nodded again.

"Except it seem like Joyce's school, management company, or whatever, is a little more earnest about really serving the community. That Thigpen talks a good game, but you and I know that he's been obstructing Elaine every chance he got.

All this bullshit about the money is really 'cause he mad Elaine outsmarted him."

"You damn sure got that right," Cleve responded.

"But here is the thing Cleve - me, you, Joyce, Stokely, Song, all of us know that the job is Elaine's driving force, her purpose."

Cleve continued to nod in agreement.

"Me and Joyce are planning to persuade Elaine to spend some time over at Joyce's school." Francine paused to see if Cleve was following her thoughts. When she saw that he was, she continued, "If we get her back in the mix, whether part-time or volunteering, we think we can get her purpose juices following again. You know, help her get her fire back."

Cleve leaned back in his chair, folded one arm across his chest, and stroked his chin with the other hand. "Yeah, y'all might be on to something ..."

"That skating y'all did? That was a big deal. Almost like the spark to get things going. You gotta keep that up and you gotta work on her a little bit here and there to get her to accept Joyce's invitation."

There was a moment of silence as they both pondered the 'or else' idea that both were too scared to verbalize.

18

PEOPLE WHO ARE DARKER THAN BLUE

Curtis Mayfield

Tuesday, December 3, 2013

"*P*rincipal Robeson ain't nuthin' but a hater," Judah Johnson stated as he leaned back in his chair.

The comment took everyone by surprise.

Board member Armstrong Thomas was rendered momentarily speechless at Mr. Johnson's declaration. Yet, he pushed forward with his questioning, "Can you elaborate on what you mean by 'hater'?"

"Everybody know she a hater, man. Er'body." Mr. Johnson did a sweeping motion with his open palm as if his statement was final.

Board Member McLeod assumed the questioning. "Did you ever participate in the Saturday Sessions?"

"Hell nawl. My baby mama be going to that shit," Judah said with a sneer as he rolled his eyes in Elaine's direction. He resumed, "You can always tell when she go to, because she be talking all that 'be a leader in your household,' shit."

Board Member Sharif framed his words as a question but

it wasn't. "Mr. Johnson, can you refrain from the profanity, brother?"

"Yeah, dawg. Like I said, she a hater."

Cleve's jaws tightened and he stood slowly. He didn't say anything. He narrowed his glare onto Judah Johnson.

Mr. Johnson continued his tough charade by talking trash from the stand, "Man, sit yo' old ass down. Ain't nobody scared of you."

Sharif inserted more firmly, "Brother Johnson."

"Man, all y'all tripping! She the one stealing the money and y'all ackin' all brand new and shit."

Although Reverend Thigpen was enjoying this testimony against Principal Robeson, but even he knew Johnson was getting out of line. Thigpen slammed the gavel, "Young man, this is a public hearing. We will practice decorum." He even pointed the gavel at Johnson and peered a displeased expression from over the rim of his glasses.

Judah Johnson flapped from side to side in his chair like a spoiled child.

Attorney Mankiller whispered for Cleve to take a seat and then approached the stand. "You said, 'be a leader in your household.' What does that mean?"

Judah folded his arms. "It means when you get a bunch of women together all they gonna do is blame men. That's why I call the school 'Playahataville,' 'cause they just hate on the dads and ..." He was going to say "Shit" but Sharif's throat clearing reminded him not too.

Attorney Mankiller urged him on, "You take offense to being a leader in your home?"

Johnson was confused by the question. The confusion was frozen on his face. He resorted to his familiar position, "Look all I know is when my baby mama spend a Saturday in Playahataville, the next thing I know the judge is raising my child support."

Mankiller was toying with him, "They make you pay child support for a child in your home?"

"What?," Johnson retorted.

"JJ, that's what they call you right?" Mankiller didn't wait for his response, "I never heard of making child support payments for a child living at home."

"Lil' Jay don't live with me. He stay wit' my baby's mama's mama."

"His grandmother?"

"Yeah, that's what I said."

"Do you have joint custody or visitation rights?"

"Nah. Well, not yet."

"Yet?"

"See, you a hater too."

"What?"

"All y'all bit ... um, ladies, yeah all y'all be hatin' on a brother on the come up!"

Mr. Johnson' testimony was both sad and absurd. It was apparent that he built a fortress around his ignorance and shook his saber of immaturity at anyone who trespassed upon his ego.

Sharif seized the questioning, "Brother Johnson, what is your relationship with Ella Baker Academy? Are you an involved parent?"

"Man, I ain't got time for that," Johnson responded as if annoyed.

A hush over took the audience.

Sharif was puzzled; yet, through his bewilderment, he asked, "Why are you here Brother Johnson?"

Everyone in the audience leaned closer to hear his answer.

He noticed, sat back, stroked his chin, and said confidently, "I ain't no snitch."

Some in the audience threw up their hands in disbelief.

Armstrong Thomas added a question, "Mr. Johnson, are

you aware that this is a public hearing to decipher the integrity of Principal Robeson?"

Judah Johnson did not respond, verbally. Instead, he pursed his lips and turned them upward.

Attorney Mankiller petitioned the board, "Can we call our next parent as Mr. Johnson doesn't have anything else to say."

Johnson roared in response, "Oh, I got a lot to say. A whole damn lot to say! Not only is Principal Robeson stealing the money, she cheating on them state tests, and making up numbers on count day!"

Murmurs of disbelief boomeranged through the audience.

"Objection!" shouted Mankiller. "This is not the place for rumor or innuendo. Mr. Johnson, you cannot make unsubstantiated claims in this forum."

"Unsubstantiated? I know it's true"

"How? What proof?"

"Rev told me."

The auditorium was overcome with a hush of silence.

19

SMILING FACES SOMETIMES

The Undisputed Truth

Sunday, December 8, 2013

Morning service was the finale of the weekend-long pastoral anniversary celebration for Reverend Amos Thigpen. Reverend Jericho Daniels, pastor of The Greater Temple of the True Gospel, was the keynote speaker.

As Reverend Daniels took the podium, he smiled and winked at his wife, Delores, and mouthed 'Thank you' to his wife's friend, Denise and Denise's daughter, Phoenix. First Lady Daniels was there to support her husband. Denise was there to support her friend and college roommate, Delores; and Phoenix was there as Denise's chauffeur.

After the preliminary formalities, Reverend Daniels asked, "If you brought your bibles, can you turn to James chapter one, verse eight." He waited a moment before inserting a joke, "For those of you unaccustomed to using your bibles, if you turn almost to back, you'll be just about there." A few chuckles came from the congregation.

"The Word of the God informs us that 'A double minded

man is unstable in all his ways.'" To signal that he was ready to proceed with his sermon, he asked, "May the Lord add a blessing for the reading of his word."

With a deep sigh and a look of cheerful expression, Reverend Daniels began, "When I was a boy, there were two pretty girls in my class, Latrice and Joi, and let me tell you, all of us boys had our hopes to make one of them or maybe even both of them our girlfriend." He paused for a moment to survey the congregation before continuing, "One day, I told my daddy about my predicament. Like any good father, he listened to me weigh the pros and cons of each of girl before asking him who should I pursue." Daniels took a moment to wipe his mouth with his handkerchief before adding, "I was assuming that they even knew who I was, but nevertheless my father looked at me and asked seriously, 'Now you say you like Latrice and Joi?' And I agreed very quickly and happily that yes I liked both of Latrice and Joi. To which my father told me, he said, 'Son if you like both 'em then you don't love neither one of them."

A handful of "Amens!" were shouted from the congregation.

Daniels continued, "Church let me tell you, that when it came to those girls, I was a double-minded boy." The church laughed as he went on, "I was unstable in my affections." The laughter grew louder.

"It wasn't until the Lord blessed me with my wife that I became singular in my focus. Wasn't no more double-mindedness, First Lady Daniels started within my spirit a single minded purpose!"

The congregation was cracking-up with laughter. Delores was blushing from pride and embarrassment.

"Saints, I'm not the only single-minded preacher in this pulpit. Lord knows I ain't. We are here to celebrate the ministry and leadership of a single-minded servant of the Lord, Reverend Amos Thigpen!"

A roar of applause filled the sanctuary.

At a glance, Denise appeared to be paying full attention to the sermon. However, just out of sight of the other parishoners she texted her daughter.

Denise: We about to be here all day.

Phoenix, who had yet to master her mother's poker face, responded to the buzz from her phone, read the text, and began laughing. She was nearly convincing in covering up her amusement by capping it with well-timed 'Amen' and some clapping. Much like a person who stumbles a bit while walking then attempts to convert the stumble into a slight jog.

This was happening as Reverend Daniels was heaping praise onto Reverend Thigpen much like a farmer bales hay. Persons with an eye for such things could see Thigpen's head swelling and chest expanding from such effusive ego-stroking.

Phoenix: How many more adjectives is he going to heap on the man?

Denise: Just until that stuffed turkey explodes like a watermelon.

They both laughed. Delores missed their delight as she was standing with her hands clasped together and rocking from side-to-side as if her husband's gratuitous praise of Thigpen were a spiritual revelation.

Denise: You know he is the ring leader of the group trying to oust that principal.

Phoenix: Wait. What?

Denise: You do watch the news, don't you?

Phoenix: C'mon mom. I get tired of hearing what's wrong with the world.

"Preach Reverend!" Denise shouted as she waved one hand in the air before resuming her texting.

Denise: The charter school scandal. They have brought charges against the CFO for stealing money but the principal they are accusing of stealing spent money for computers and spent it on weekend tutoring and lunch programs for the kids.

Phoenix: Did she pocket any of the money?

Denise: Not a cent. Even those like Reverend Big Head up there that want her fired acknowledge that she didn't profit.

Phoenix: So what's the problem? Shouldn't they just reprimand her and keep it moving?

Denise: That's what I think. But some folks trying to milk it for all the publicity they can.

Reverend Daniels was reaching his crescendo, "When a singled-minded man, fueled by the word of the Lord, is focused on improving the education for the children of Detroit, let no man or woman stand in his way!"

Phoenix: Did Daniels just take a shot at the principal?

Denise: You better believe it.

Phoenix: That's petty. I thought this was church.

Denise: Now Phoenix, you know everybody in the church ain't got the church in them. And that includes the preachers.

Phoenix: Especially the preachers.

Denise: Can I get an amen?

Phoenix: Amen mama!

Denise: Now it's time for offering.

Phoenix: LOL!!

Reverend Daniels then announced the lie that ministers often tell, "Saints, just give me a five more minutes to tell you how the Lord is doing a mighty work through Reverend Thigpen!"

Denise: That means we gonna be here another hour.

Phoenix: MOM!! LOL LOL LOL!!!!!

OPEN OUR EYES

Earth, Wind & Fire

Tuesday, December 10, 2013

To gaze upon Bart Peters was to see the shell of a man with a hollowed-out soul. Mr. Peters was a sergeant and twenty-one year veteran with the Detroit Police Department. He began his career with an optimism that colored his dreams of being a change agent. However, life and the job has dulled those colors into a morass of grey.

Board member Sharif began questioning with a reminder of the first smudge against the hopeful colors of Sergeant Peters' police ambitions.

"Weren't you one of those officers who killed Malice Green?" asked Sharif as he was sorted through his vast recollections of police injustice.

Peters' eyes rolled up into his head and he exhaled a long defeated sigh, "Noooo, I was not one of the officers who engaged Mr. Green. I was a rookie officer assigned to the same precinct as the officers who assaulted Mr. Green." Then Peters sat more erect and added a question of his own, "Does my job have something to do with Principal Robeson?"

Sharif smirked like a chess player who is one move away from placing his opponent in checkmate, "Actually it does."

Everyone in the auditorium leaned forward to hear how the matters were related.

With a captive audience, Sharif went off on a tangent. "It matters because you are a public servant who, I don't know, maybe contributed to an attempt to cover up a crime against the people and today we are expected to trust your word regarding another public servant who may have committed a crime against the people." Sharif sat back as if he had actually executed the checkmate.

Sergeant Peters was not phased, "You know Brother Sharif, it's a lot of y'all out there kicking up sand about the people but y'all track record of actually doing something substantial is suspect." Peters tetter-tottered his flat palm gesture to accentuate his point. The two engaged in a brief stare down before Peters resumed his testimony, "For over twenty years I've been sacrificing my life so that the citizens of Detroit can feel safe. You think I get some type of pride in arresting broken-spirited and bitter people? Those thugs need healing while at the same time our community needs protecting. What do you want me to do? Complain about what's wrong in Detroit or roll up my sleeves and get to the business of protecting Detroit."

Sharif nodded his head slowly. This match of egos would have to wait for another day as Board chairperson Van Vetchen refocused the questioning. "Sergeant Peters, what is your connection with Ella Baker Academy?"

"My twin daughters, Faith and Hope, are seventh graders there. They've been there since third grade."

Board member McLeod inserted, "Have you or your daughters ever participated in the Saturday Sessions?"

"My wife and daughters have participated. My wife has been bed-ridden since February and between taking care of her, the girls, and the job, I just couldn't keep up with the schedule. So, no, I have never been but I have an idea about what goes on there."

Board member Thomas asked, "What did your wife and daughters say about it?"

"Well, my wife was kind of in-and-out of the little parent meetings. She thought it was good but that she didn't need that kind of help. The girls? They didn't really like the idea of school on a Saturday but the teachers and their friends made it something they looked forward to."

McLeod interjected, "What do you mean by 'that kind of help'?"

"Maybe it's just me and my wife, but we was thinking the whole Saturday thing was for poor people or single mothers." Peters thought a second about what he said and then backpedaled a bit, "Not that anything is wrong with poor people and single mothers, my sister is a single mother. But we didn't need that kind of help."

McLeod followed with, "So why bring your girls?"

"It was free. Plus the more time they spend learning helps them get a little more prepared to get into Cass or Renaissance."

Peters' response gave the board members pause. The implication that an Ella Baker education extended beyond its campus had been overlooked during these hearings. Attending and graduating from either Cass or Renaissance carried the perception of a certain accelerated trajectory for its students.

The silence caused by their pause prompted Sergeant Peters to resume speaking to cover what he assumed was a misunderstanding. "Everybody knows that more than likely if your kid is at a DPS middle school, there may be forty to fifty kids in a room with a substitute teacher and possibly no books. Hannah and I thought Baker Academy would be a better option. Plus now considering her health care costs, Baker being tuition-free helps our family's bottom line. The allegations against Principal Robeson not withstanding, we have always been satisfied, in fact, we still love the quality teaching and family atmosphere at Baker."

McLeod thanked him and added, "Quality teaching and family atmosphere are essential to the success of this school ..." Reverend Thigpen interrupted before the praise could become too gratuitous, "... And we believe ethical leadership is also essential."

His interruption garnered more than a handful of side-eye glances, arm-folding, and slow exhales of exasperation from listeners. For those who were slow to notice, it was becoming apparent that Reverend Thigpen had a vendetta against Principal Robeson. The thought was troubling for all who contemplated it as none of them could fathom a legitimate reason as to why. Additionally, they could not reconcile that a man of the cloth could be such an asshole.

21

THE GREATEST LOVE OF ALL

George Benson

Wednesday, December 11, 2013

*B*uilding Beautiful Daughters was far from one of those run-of-mill nonprofit organizations, where good intentions are undercut by leaders whose satisfaction is derived from saying what they will do instead of consistently doing what they promised. Building Beautiful Daughters exemplified the can-do and will-do spirit of its founder, Phoenix Ellison.

People do not typically create nonprofits to generate wealth. Most do it out of a sense of service. Phoenix's compulsory sense of service was so strong, her life revolved around BBD, which made the circumstances a bit of a paradox - she was not doing it for the money, but she needed the money from doing it.

Since its inception, BBD has been a one-woman show with occasional part-time help. Every development program that serviced a Girl Scout Troop, youth ministry, or school program was conducted by Phoenix. Her 2014 goal of expansion hinged on starting the year with at least one of the two potential contracts. She had a preliminary meeting with Principal Clarence Wilkins at Shuttlesworth Elementary School on January 8th and Principal Joyce Keys at Tubman Technical Academy on January 23rd.

Additionally, her pet project of creating a book about Detroit's decaying architecture made her add a visit to the local university's School of Architecture on the first Monday in January, to her list of priorities.

While the idea of publishing a book was inspiring and her goals with BBD were dear to her heart, Phoenix had another goal that she wouldn't dare mention aloud. She wanted to be in a healthy, reciprocal, love relationship with future promise.

She hoped to replace the irritation that accompanied every social media visit that revealed an engagement, wedding, baby shower, or anniversary announcement. She was happy for her friends but wanted to share some good news about her life beyond BBD. If she were in a healthy relationship, Phoenix believed that the friendship would fill the growing void in her personal life.

When she graduated from Bennett College, she and her friends had idealistic goals of changing the world. The reality of the work required to change the world frightened each of them. Phoenix and a few others chose graduate school as an incubator for their potential as they figured out more precisely how they would make their dreams work; some coupled newly minted BA and BS degrees with a more personal MRS degree that was accompanied with a wedding ring. However, in the years that have passed since commencement, real life has weighed on the bonds they shared and decreased their interactions to social media messages.

The young professional network in Detroit provided some cool acquaintances and even a few dating opportunities; however, none of them measured up to the love hopes she carried in her heart. It wasn't that she wasn't approached by men or women that discouraged her; instead it was who she was approached by: the big-plans-but-no-results brother, the entitled pretty boy, the competing / you-can't-outshine-me dude, the money-over-everything egotist, the overbearing - I'm-going-to-convert-you lesbian, the god-said-women-have-their-place guy, the immaculately-groomed-other-ethnicity fetishizer of Black women, the can-I-stay-with-you-'til-I-get-on-my-feet moocher, and a host of other underwhelming options.

She had anticipated that dating as a professional woman would be more promising but too many of her nights were as cold and gloomy as Detroit winters.

In a bit of optimism and self-reflection, she murmured a prayer to the ancestors, releasing anything that she may be holding onto that was obstructing her opportunities for real love and with that she figured 2014 was going to be her year.

22

DON'T MAKE ME OVER

Dionne Warwick

Friday, December 13, 2013

*E*laine was intercepted.

Following an evening of skating with Cleve, the couple found another pair awaiting them in the skating rink parking lot - Joyce and Francine.

While leaning on the hood of Cleve's Cadillac DTS with her head cocked to one side and an aggressive finger pointing gesture, Francine shouted in her dramatic way, "Yo' ass comin' with us."

Cleve and Elaine were frozen in their tracks, then stole a glance over to Joyce, before looking back at Francine. Simultaneously, all four of them erupted in laughter.

Elaine ran into the open-armed embrace of her friends. Cleve took a moment to appreciate Elaine's joviality before needlessly shouting, "Y'all take care of my baby and don't have too much fun!"

Joyce responded, "Cleve, you know we gonna take care of our sister."

They waved "goodbye" before Cleve headed off without

his co-pilot. He was praying that tonight's intervention with her girlfriends would fortify Elaine's spirit before her upcoming testimony. He viewed himself as a lifeguard, keeping Elaine from going under in the dark waters of despondency. But it would require some extra hands to pull her out of those waters. Cleve couldn't think of better hands than Francine and Joyce.

JOYCE DROVE WITH ELAINE RIDING SHOTGUN.

Francine sat in the back with her face perched between the front seats like an over-excited child without a seatbelt.

"If you would've told me back in college that you and Cleve would still be together I woulda laughed my ass off!" Francine shouted with mirth.

Joyce added, "We were listening with disbelief when you kept talking about your boyfriend back home."

Francine jumped in with a cynical tone, "Yeah, sure you gotta a boyfriend."

Elaine enjoyed the chiding as she added, "I tried to tell y'all he was the one, but y'all didn't believe me."

"Shit, I ain't believe you until him and Columbus showed up on campus," then nudging Joyce, Francine asked, "Remember that?"

Joyce explained, "How could I forget? Those fraternity boys thought they could take advantage of us ..."

Francine interrupted, "Take advantage of y'all. They wasn't gonna do shit to me."

Elaine added, "That's bullshit Francine. You the one got us mixed up with those fools anyway."

Joyce asked one of those questions that a person knows the answer to but presents it in a way to move the conversation along, "Wasn't it Central State's homecoming or something?"

Francine took the conversation and ran. "Them fools thought we was impressed..."

Elaine cut her off, "We wouldn't of been there if you weren't trying to 'eat and drink for free.'"

"Well exCUUUUUUUUSSSSSe me Miss I-Want-To-Stay-In-The-Dorm-While-Everybody-Else- Parties!"

Joyce shared, "Yeah, Elaine, we always did have to drag you out the dorm. What was up with that?"

Francine inserted, "What I want to know is how in the hell did Cleve and them know where we were?"

"I always called him on Saturdays at 6pm and since we were waiting on you to get dressed ..." Elaine allowed the silence to convey the established truth of the length of time it takes for Francine to get dressed. Joyce laughed hard at the implication.

"So I told him we were walking over to State and, well, how could I know they were going to drive down?" Elaine shrugged her shoulders at the memory.

Joyce picked up the story, "But who in the hell did those jackasses think they were by slinging us over their shoulders like some damn cavemen?"

Francine sighed "Yeah, Greeks and athletes get away with all kinda ill behavior and some of the little girls be impressed."

Joyce and Elaine shared a shocked glance before stating in unison, "You was one of those impressed little girls!"

"I was." Francine smirked conspiratorially. "I figured once I whupped this good loving on them, they would be hooked for life."

Joyce said, "Well ... how did that approach work for you?"

Francine stuck up her middle finger in the rear view mirror as she veered the conversation backed to Cleve. "I shole didn't 'spect for Cleve and Columbus to be waiting outside the gym though."

Joyce mimicked Cleve's baritone, "Say Blood, those ladies are with us."

The three of them laughed at the memory.

Francine added, "I'm not sure if it was Cleve's Jim Brown impersonation or the pistol that Columbus had in his waistband, but whatever it was, them muthfuckas put us down."

Joyce was laughing when she added, "Then on some ole Shaft shit, Elaine runs over to Cleve and he raised the Black Power fist to the fraternity guys, talking about "Right On.""

The laughter continued as they reminisced that they were never approached inappropriately during the rest of their time at Wilberforce. A truth that Francine reframed as, "I never could lock down no man after Cleve pulled that stunt. He scared 'em all off!"

1:30 am, Saturday, December 14, 2013
Motor City Casino Lounge

"HEAR US OUT ELAINE, WHY NOT DO A LITTLE volunteering at our schools?" Joyce asked as she and Francine looked to their friend for an answer.

Elaine allowed a long sigh to escape, "I, I …. I don't know."

Francine retorted matter-of-factly, "Those damn charges? Shit, you got them. You're gonna beat them. But then what? You want that principal job back after how they trying to do you?"

Joyce gave a slight slow-down gesture that Elaine did not see as she faced Francine. "Francine is right, you are going to beat those allegations. I mean, maybe you could sue them for libel or something. But, what we are saying is even when you win the case, you've already lost Ella Baker Academy."

Elaine let out another long sigh while shaking her head.

"But lookahere, that damn school don't make you! Shit, what they call it …" Francine snapped her fingers twice before the term came to mind. "You have …" she switched to a mock-corporate tone, "transferable skills." Then she nudged Joyce, who returned a wink. "You can take your leadership skills to any school and the kids and families would love you!"

"Yeah, but …" another sigh. "I'm not sure if it's in me anymore."

The sadness in her eyes stole a bit of her friends' hope.

"Remember, all we had to go through just to get administrative interviews?" Francine and Joyce nodded knowingly.

"People were stuck in antiquated ideas that women could only teach. It didn't matter that we had the experience and credentials, we had to put up with the narrow-mindedness of lesser talented male principals."

"Amen" Francine and Joyce added.

"Then we got our chance and the economy went … splut!" Elaine accompanied the sound with a mean face and thumbs down gesture. "Mayor Young used to say 'If America got a cold then Detroit got pneumonia!' But, it took that for us to get some real chances to lead more departments and a couple of schools."

Francine interjected, "I never will forget when we was at Brady Elementary in the 80s when kids started working for YBI!"

Joyce shook her head, "Young Boys Incorporated … who could forget them?"

Elaine's cynicism responded, "Shit, who created them? Ronald Reagan and his ilk."

"What?!" Francine shrieked before retorting, "Ronald damn Reagan ain't made them hoodlums sell drugs!"

"Nawl, he helped take the jobs out the city so that selling drugs was the new economy," Elaine shot back.

Francine threw up her hands.

Joyce interceded, "But, that's the whole point, you been through a lot and given a lot to this city and its kids." She paused to be sure Elaine was listening. "But as your friend, I'm not sure how long you can go on without doing what you love."

"That's why I'm retiring."

Both Francine and Joyce were slack-jawed.

The bartender stopped and was going to ask if they would be needing any more drinks.

"Yeah, another round," Francine replied before the bartender could finish her question.

Joyce held up both hands, open-palmed. "We're not asking you to take another principal job. We're just asking, would you consider volunteering at our schools until you figure out what you want to do next ?"

Francine jumped in, "She means volunteer at her school 'cause you swore you wasn't never stepping foot back in a Detroit Public School and since I'm still with DPS ..." She smirked and pointed her finger at Joyce, "You need to think about volunteering with her."

Joyce jumped in before Elaine could say anything, "Serving the community is who you are, it's your lifeline. You could be the principal, teacher, or superintendent - but whatever you do, you have to serve. It's all I've ever known you to do."

Elaine nodded in agreement.

Francine pointed her finger and was going to interject, Joyce waved her down and continued, "I got a meeting with this nonprofit about programming for our girls. We're going to get together in about a month to hash it out. But, the thing is, while I know their program is good for the school, the little lady director - well, I want to be sure she can really hang. I want to have someone with her until she gets going real good."

Elaine pondered a bit before replying, "And that someone is me?"

Francine couldn't stay muted for long, "Why not you? Can you tell us someone better?" She took a quick sip of wine before adding, "'Specially if you retiring and shit, you'll have the time!"

Elaine did not answer, but in her mind she was picturing how it could work.

23

YOU MAKE ME FEEL BRAND NEW

The Stylistics

Tuesday, December 17, 2013

*A*ndrette Thomas had been through deeper waters than this. She survived Hurricane Katrina and the bombing of the levees that gave way to the submersion of her community. Those rising waters pushed Andrette ashore, anew.

Prior to Katrina, the people in her parish knew Andrette as Andrew. Just as the storm washed away the world he had known, Katrina also leveled the above-ground crypt within which he concealed his burgeoning need to be liberated from social constructs. The chaos, fear, and grief that made the local arena an inhospitable shelter, also proved to be the soil from which the seed of opportunity began blooming into a different life, with a new name, new identity, and new gender.

One aspect of the new identity of a former introverted adolescent boy was that of a young adult woman who served as the cafeteria manager for Ella Baker Academy. The only link to her old life in New Orleans was the gold cap on her tooth.

Andrette suffered no fools and Reverend Thigpen was a fool for riding his high horse into this interview session.

"I find it peculiar that the most unqualified and perhaps unsure of themselves would be selected to testify on Mrs. Robeson's behalf," Thigpen mockingly intoned.

Before "Objection!" could escape Attorney Mankiller's lips, Andrette replied, "Are you talking about yourself?"

Thigpen did not have a verbal response, but non-verbally, his head recoiled into his neck, his eyebrows furrowed, his lips tightened, and his countenance was angered. The audience was amused and even Elaine managed to smile.

Board member McLeod assumed the questioning, "Miss Thomas, can you tell us your relationship with Ella Baker Academy?"

"Yeah, but I gotta start a little bit before I go there," perhaps anyone else would have waited for McLeod to say "ok" but Andrette had long stopped awaiting others' approval. "I ended up in Detroit after losing my family and friends to Hurricane Katrina and FEMA. I bounced around from shelters and cheap motels before I ended up working for the temp agency that placed me at Ella just after my birthday, January 2, 2011. I was just helping in the lunchroom for four hours a day but after a couple of weeks, Principal Robeson asked if I could help with getting snacks to the after school kids. Then the weekend kids. Then she kept-on, part-time over the summer, but because I had been with the school so long the temp agency says they had to hire me and that's what Principal Robeson did. I worked the cafeteria all by myself during summer school and then the next school year I was full-time as the interim cafeteria manger."

Board member Sharif cleared his throat before asking, "What type of role model would you say you are for the students at Ella Baker?"

Few knew what Sharif really meant but Andrette chose to

play along, "I'm the type of role model that shows kids they can have the courage to be who they really are."

Sharif would not be hushed like Thigpen and he quickly quipped, "And who are you?"

"I am Andrette Thomas."

"Were you always Andrette Thomas?"

Mankiller stood to object but Andrette held up her hand as to assure that she had it under control.

"I have always been Andrette Thomas."

Sharif went on. He looked to his fellow board members and said, "While this is not relevant to this case, I want to add that I have held my tongue on my opinion that Mrs. Robeson did not empower enough black men." Before anyone could get a word in, Sharif steamrolled forward, "If you look at all the employees, we have all these women and two men, or maybe two and a half ..." he sneered at Andrette before going on, "The janitor and the gym teacher."

No one knew where he was going with all this but gave him the benefit of the doubt by listening.

"How can we really be about the business of uplifting the black community if there is no place for the black man?"

Andrette jumped in, "It's five board members and three of y'all is black men but that ain't enough for you?" Sharif shot an angry glare to Andrette who was unperturbed, "Look everybody know it ain't that many black men teaching but everybody also know that too many of y'all want to make speeches and ain't really about doing the work."

Sharif was shushed.

"Look at the churches," Andrette said this while looking directly at Reverend Thigpen, "Yeah, the pastor is a man but who doing the missionary work, who paying the tithes, who keeping all the stuff together? I'll tell you who - Mother So & So, Sister So & So, and Missionary So & So - that's who! Y'all be wanting all kinds of praise for doing stuff y'all supposed to do! Talkin' 'bout ..." Andrette took on a mocking male voice that channeled an earlier witness, Judah Johnson, "'... I pay my child support.' You supposed to do that! At least."

Armstrong Thomas said in a shaky voice, "Miss Thomas, you've made your point."

Andrette's look of disbelief could not have been more repulsed and that fueled her diatribe, "See! When it get too hot in the kitchen, y'all be trying to silence the sisters!"

Andrette's proclamation induced silence within the auditorium.

Attorney Mankiller held up both palms as if conveying she is coming with no weapons or tricks. She walked slowly to the witness stand and broke the silence by asking, "Once you became full-time, did that include working the Saturday Sessions?"

It took a moment for Miss Thomas to relinquish her defensive stance; however, when she did she replied, "Yes, the Saturday Sessions were a part of my full-time contract."

Mankiller continued, "Miss Thomas can you share your opinion on the Saturday Sessions?"

"Yeah, to me, that was like the best time. I mean, like the teachers be talking about all the testing and stuff but I think on Saturdays, that's when they really get to do their thing, you know what I mean?"

"I'm not sure, elaborate. Give us some examples of teachers 'doing their thing.'"

"Okay, so let's say Ms. Hollis right? She teaches middle school science but on Saturday, she does all these recycling and urban farming projects. I'm just going on what I hear, but I don't know if she gets to that kind of teaching with having to get the kids ready for the MEAP."

Mankiller asked, "Can you clarify what the MEAP is for those that do not know?"

"Oh yeah, that's the state test. Like as far as I can tell

different grades be having to take the MEAP on different subjects and like I was saying, Ms. Hollis gotta do her thing with that test before the fun teaching happens."

"Miss Thomas, a large part of the charges against Principal Robeson is connected to food and the cafeteria. Tell us what you know about this."

"Well, it ain't no secret that this ain't the richest neighborhood. Er'ybody know that. So like even when I first started, Principal Robeson would have me keep the left overs in a certain part of the freezer. Then the next day, it would be gone. She told me later that after school, she would wait 'til most of the kids were gone and take a few of the kids to the kitchen to load up their backpacks with the leftovers." Andrette paused after slightly choking up, "That's when Principal Robeson really became my dawg. I mean, she good people 'cause she thinking 'bout how the kids doing even after they leave the school."

"Was the food served on Saturday part of the regular school lunch menu?"

"Nah. I mean like, just so you know – I just deal with receiving the food and gettin' it to the kids; I don't know nuthin' 'bout the paying for it or what not. Anyway so like the food on Saturday came from different vendors or restaurants but unlike the regular school lunches, it wasn't never no leftovers. The kids ate er'thang!"

"Tell us how feeding the students goes on Saturday."

"You know how fancy restaurants have appetizers, entrees, and dessert? Well, like when the kids get there, they would get like the appetizers you know, something to squash the hungry feeling. Then that last forty minutes or so before they go home, they eat the entree. But wait, see, they had to eat in silence or read a book. Any book, but either read and eat or hush. I ain't never seen so many kids reading at the same time."

"So they had to read to get dessert?"

"Yeah, kinda. Not that official though, kinda like a unspoken rule."

"Can tell us about your relationship with Principal Robeson?"

"Like I said, Principal Robeson, I call her Boss Lady though, she my dawg. Not only did she get me a real job with benefits, she helped me get my GED done and start classes at Wayne County Community College."

"Are you testifying because Principal Robeson is your friend?"

"Nawl. Yo' boss ain't yo' friend, they can't be. But Boss Lady really helped me get on my feet. She gave me new life. She not only committed to the kids, she try to help er'body. She ain't my friend, she's my hero."

Some people in the audience clapped.

24

EVERY YEAR, EVERY CHRISTMAS

Luther Vandross

Thursday, December 26, 2013

*A*s has been their family tradition for twenty years, the Robesons arrived at the Huron Correction Facility at the beginning of visiting hours to celebrate the holiday with Songhai, also known as offender number 120417.

"This is the last Christmas we spend here," Elaine announced matter-of-factly.

The declaration was more than an optimistic projection, it held the affirming certainty of mother-wit and premonition.

Neither Songhai, Stokely, nor Cleve wanted to disagree, nor could they picture the circumstances that would make Songhai's release a reality.

Prison may have hardened Songhai's disposition, but, it could not quell her receptiveness to her mother's love.

After a moment or so, Cleve inserted, "Well, I guess I'm gonna get your bedroom ready in advance. You know I don't wanna be cutting it close like last time."

'Last time' was an inside joke shared between he and

Elaine. It referenced the time before Elaine returned home with a newborn Songhai. Cleve, who was still working at Dodge Main, had worked several double-time shifts so that he could keep the family finances afloat while taking time off for his new family. Perhaps it was the hormonal fluctuations that come with pregnancy that fueled Elaine's persistent requests, (or nagging as Cleve described), for him to paint the room for the baby. But, whatever the cause, Cleve couldn't find time to paint until the last minute.

Cleve did one last shift at the factory after Song's delivery and left work at 2:00 am. When he got home, he painted the room and assembled furniture from 3:00 am to 11:30 am. By noon, he was picking up his wife and daughter from the hospital. During the drive home, there was a reservation in Elaine's happiness because she figured if she got home and the baby's room wasn't ready, Cleve was going to have some serious explaining to do. Cleve knew what she was thinking and said nothing.

Elaine loved the room and after setting Songhai in the crib for the first time, turned to face a mischievously smiling Cleve, who responded, "I sure love how the sunlight hits the yellow and brightens up the whole room!"

She punched and hugged him.

AFTER HIS ANNOUNCEMENT OF, 'GETTING THE ROOM ready,' Elaine punched him again.

Songhai changed the subject, "When do you testify Ma?"

"In a couple of weeks, on January 21st."

"Ready to kick-ass?" Songhai responded.

Elaine's maternal instincts never adjusted to Songhai's profanity; however, considering her daughter's environment, Elaine chose not to speak on it.

"Yeah, if that's what you wanna call it."

The rest of the family was confused.

Cleve went first, "What's that 'posed to mean, 'Laine?"

In childish, choral unison, Songhai and Stokely added, "Yeah Ma, what's that 'sposed to mean?"

"I'm retiring." Elaine collected herself to continue with words she had never previously verbalized to her family. "No matter the outcome, I will not take another principal job." With that, Elaine drew her line in the sand.

Her family had various memories of when she reached a similar conclusion about Detroit Public Schools. They knew there was no changing her mind. But, they wanted to know how she ended up here and what was she going to do next.

Cleve was especially worrying because he had hoped that Joyce and Francine could sway Elaine; but now, he was wondering if Friday night's orchestrated get-together would bear any fruit.

Sensing her family's confusion, Elaine continued, "This isn't the first time I've been lied on and probably won't be the last. But GOTDAMMIT!" She pounded the table. Everyone in the visiting room looked in the Robeson's direction. Two of guards moved closer. Cleve sort of waved them off, silently gesturing that things were okay.

Elaine was seething at the recollection of the past few months and was despondently angry at the unfairness of it all. "Why must I be vilified for serving? All I've done was help people. I've even been underpaid and overworked, but did anyone have something to say then? Noooooooooo, it's all good, as long as Principal Robeson keeps slaving away!"

Then what seemed like something Cleve would say, came from Songhai's mouth, "Ma, there was this carpenter dude back in day and er'body was praising him and shit on Sunday, but by Friday, his ass was on the cross."

After the meaning of Songhai's statement set in, Stokely

began to laugh at her choice of words. "'Carpenter dude? Sis! I ain't never heard it like that!"

Cleve jumped in, "That don't change its truth." Then he high-fived Songhai.

If they were still children, Songhai would have stuck her tongue out at Stokely, but as adults, she gave him a look that said "Yeah, what Dad said."

"You just gonna give up on schools?" Stokely asked.

Elaine shrugged her shoulders, "Joyce and Francine practically cornered me to volunteer at Joyce's school." She shrugged again, "I don't know, I might help Joyce a little bit." Then with a faraway glance, "But, after that, I really don't know."

25

BREAK UP TO MAKE UP

The Stylistics

Friday, December 27, 2013

"*S*TOKELY!!"

With a quick kicking back of the covers and a hop to his feet, Stokely rushed into the bathroom from where he heard Tanya scream. Deep down he wanted to laugh but he knew that would make a bad thing worse.

What he saw was Tanya angrily siting down in the toilet. She was fuming because Stokely had forgotten to put the seat down.

What he couldn't know was that Tanya had been deliberating or more accurately, stewing for some time. Her stewing anger was the fostering of the animosity she would need to break things off with Stokely. In her heart, she did not want their dalliance to end. Why would she? She had the best of both worlds: a wealthy, supportive husband who resided in Nashville and a love nest with a younger, captivating man in Detroit.

However, she carried tremendous guilt. She felt guilty for cheating on her husband. She felt guilty because she knew

Stokely's emotional attachment to her was growing stronger and that he may soon want to change the terms of their relationship. But, most of all, she felt guilty because she was beginning to love Stokely. If she were totally honest with herself, she had long loved Stokely but, periodically, Tanya would shroud truth with denial - particularly if those truths were about herself.

Toilet water is usually cool, yet the anger Tanya was fostering toward Stokely not only heated her, it could have also boiled the toilet water.

Stokely extended his hand to help her to her feet. He held back his laughter as he recalled memories from the movie, *The Wiz*, where the witch falls down into a toilet. Tanya was no witch, however, she was six feet tall and the contrast from her usual commanding presence to this scene of being stuck in the toilet was an extreme shift in Stokely's perception.

She shooed his hand away.

He instead reached for a towel.

"What are you getting that for?!" she screamed.

He couldn't hold his laughter any longer, "I want to help dry your ass off."

"I still have to pee, get out!"

With that, he tossed the towel near the toilet and left the room.

Moments after the toilet flushed and the faucet ran, Tanya stormed into their bedroom.

"I find it real funny how you forget something and it costs me!" She said while pointing a finger at him and then to herself.

Stokely did not say a word. He used his energy to stop laughing.

"All that damn intelligence and you forget to put the seat down! It just doesn't make any sense." She threw both hands up in disbelief. Her anger blocked the reality that she was naked and carrying on in front of man who tremendously admired the view. He really could not hear her anger about the toilet or the conjuring she was doing to justify leaving him. He sat on the edge of the bed transfixed by the movement of her breasts during her tantrum.

She was right though. This was not his first time leaving the seat up. He would be eternally unsuccessful in conveying that his forgetfulness was directly related to his eagerness to return to bed. The intimate synergy they shared was so exceptional, that while most men shun snuggling, Stokely was more than happy to partake. Not because it led to sex, but because they slept in the nude and their blissful intertwining made sleeping through the night the highlight of many of their days.

However, "I forgot I left the seat up because I couldn't wait to get back to you," sounds childish, so Stokely left that unsaid.

Tanya noticed that her rant had no effect on Stokely. She also noticed how he was taking in her body. Her husband, Oscar, looked at her in a similar way. The look initially triggered feelings of insecurity that were followed by a bit of affirming self-talk. Talk that assured her of the power of her presence.

That acknowledgement began to release the steam from her anger. It also prompted her to hold her pose a little longer to tantalize Stokely further. She knew she was going to leave. She also knew that it would be more sooner than later. Yet, the way Stokely's admiration made her feel, she knew she wasn't leaving tonight.

YOU, ME, & HE

Mtume

Wednesday, January 1, 2014

*T*anya brought in the New Year with her husband, Oscar, and his friends in Nashville.

In Tanya's eyes, it was a gathering of old stiffs and their well-preserved wives.

In Oscar's eyes, it was another day closer to when he would execute his well-developed plan of moving his wife permanently to Nashville. His conniving mind blinded him to the reality that she was out place in this part of his world. This social setting consisted of nine couples of which they were the only African-Americans. While some women would adore the lavish styling of Tanya's locs, these affluent, elderly White women did not know what to make of the style. Their inquires and impulses to touch her hair were met with a silent menacing glare.

In addition to being the only African-American woman in attendance, Tanya was one of the youngest, being matched in age by the hosting couple's son. She was also so the tallest. Among the women, she was also the only one who held a job

- by choice, as Oscar frequently reminded her. Indeed, Oscar's net worth and earnings meant that Tanya did not have to work; however, considering her upbringing in southwest Detroit and how her mother instilled in her the karmic obligation to pay it forward, Tanya worked because she chose too. Her choice, her job, and her world; however, in this world, she felt out of place.

"Mrs. Rousseau, that is the most unique hairstyle. Your people are so creative, whatever do you call that style?"

Tanya was incensed. As her blood pressure rose, she spotted Oscar guffawing heartily with a few of his cronies while staring at her. She could tell that his laughter was contrived and his smiles were plastic. Despite their years of marriage, she never understood why he chose company such as this.

"It's cultural, Mrs. Vanderbilt, we refer to them as locs" Tanya replied as she stealthily stepped away from Mrs. Vanderbilt's attempt to touch.

"Cultural? Are you Jamaican?"

The southwest Detroit part of her thought, "Bitch what!?" But Mrs. Rousseau's controlled response was, "You do know that Jamaicans and others from the Caribbean are a part of the African Diaspora? My locs are a tribute to my heritage." Tanya's smile was sinister and she emphasized her height advantage by stepping closer and towering over Mrs. Vanderbilt.

Both ladies were startled as Oscar stepped into the standoff with a gentle hand to Tanya's elbow, "Excuse me Vivian, I need to borrow my wife." He shared a plastic smile and began talking to Tanya as they walked away, "Darling you have to see these pictures of Hal and Archie's new development." Oscar sincerely wanted to his wife to see the development into which he was going to invest, while also hoping to rescue her from any possible confrontations.

When they were out of earshot of Mrs. Vanderbilt, Oscar whispered, "Dear, you're acting like there is somewhere else you would rather be." He allowed the statement to linger as he extended his hand to Archie, "You guys have met my wife; by all means, show her the new project we're working on."

Oscar was not physically abusive, but in the span of thirty seconds, Tanya felt the equivalent of two slaps to the face. Does Oscar's allusion to 'Somewhere she would rather be' mean he knows about Stokely? And this project that his friends were going to show, was this additional evidence of her unawareness of the breadth and depth of her husband's financial reach? As she feigned marvel when Archie showed her the architect's renderings on his smartphone, she continued her charade by acting like an inquisitive student when Archie, Hal, and Oscar explained certain components of the rendering. In her mind, she recalled Stokely giving a more detailed explanation of one the renderings he had drawn. She then allowed the pleasure she felt in a memory of her man to coalesce with her expressions, so that her present company would think her responses were sincere.

If anyone were to inquire deeply about Tanya and Oscar's living arrangement, the subterranean truth was that Tanya found comfort in the financial security and related provisions Oscar provided, while often feeling like an accessory in his life. Oscar's deeper truth was that spiritually, his marriage to Tanya was a type of penance, an atonement for his abandonment of his first wife and their daughter. The shared truth was that theirs was a marriage of two independent souls conforming to societal expectations. It was as if their true belief was 'Since I'm supposed to be married, I may as well be married to you.' While they shared some emotional bonds, very few would wish to emulate their love.

27

KNOCKS ME OFF MY FEET

Stevie Wonder

Tuesday, January 7, 2014

Once she closed the door to her loft, Phoenix leaned back on it and slid down to the floor.

Minutes ago, she acted on her goal of visiting the School of Architecture. She figured it to be a long shot and had assumed if she met anyone it would be a gruff, old man with a heavy wool tweed jacket that had oversized patches on the elbows. Instead, she met Stokely Robeson.

It was all she could do to not melt like candle wax under his gaze. The way he was looking at her, all interested, all transfixed on what she was saying ... all tasty looking with his fine self - she truly had a moist panty moment.

She was fanning herself as she sat in her loft that was only lighted by the streetlights from the parking lot. While fanning, she reflectively analyzed his strong handshake and his caring inquiries about her proposed book. Then with the suddenness of a light bulb turning on, she remembered that he said he would work with her - YES! Her panties were re-moistened. His exact words were "Use me as you see fit" - oh,

Oh OH! How she wanted to use him alright. Damn! Right there in that little ass office. She was sure that Stokely was going to replace Idris Elba in her dreams tonight. Yet, unlike Idris, Stokely was obtainable; a real person within her world, within her reach.

She had to see him again!

She looked at the clock, she had about two hours to freshen up before meeting her book collaborators, Pedro and Jake at Slow's Bar-Be-Que. She so desperately wanted to bask in the memories of her meeting with Professor Robeson. She wanted to revisit every word, every gesture, every laugh, and everything unsaid. She needed to review and analyze the interaction to make Stokely real, to re-manifest him in reality as quickly as possible. There was no way for her to foresee how the ancestors were aligning things.

STOKELY WAS EMOTIONALLY TORN AS HE MADE HIS WAY TO Slow's.

Tanya's text to meet him there rendered him anxious.

The letter from Tanya's husband that he found in the apartment made him angry.

The love butterflies in the background of his emotions that stemmed from meeting Phoenix was a completely different matter. She was captivating. While nothing in her body language conveyed that she was flirting or even interested in him, there was something there. Something that he wouldn't be able to see clearly until he reconciled his circumstances with Tanya. He knew about the adages of rebound relationships but quite frankly, he knew his relationship with Tanya would end, so if he moved on - that couldn't technically be called rebounding, could it?

He headed to Slow's to gain closure on a love relationship

that had expired, but he was already imagining about a love relationship that could be.

Hope for the future, anguish over the present, and lessons from the past would not only prove to be his emotional make-up for this evening, but also a configuration of feelings of which he would become well-accustomed.

28

YOU BRING ME JOY

Anita Baker

Saturday, January 11, 2014

"*M*ama!!" Phoenix yelled excitedly.

The commotion caused her mother's Rottweiler, BooBaby, to go into a barking frenzy.

Denise had just stepped out of the shower. Although seeing her daughter was always a delight, she had actually planned an early bedtime tonight. So much for that.

Phoenix knocked on the bathroom door with the urgency of a five-year-old who has to pee.

"Phoenix, honey! One second!" Denise shouted from the other side.

Boo Baby leapt up and put his paws on Phoenix's shoulder as if nudging her to share the good news. Phoenix was hugging Boo Baby when Denise snatched open the door.

What she saw warmed her soul. Her only child's eyes were wide with excitement and her dog seemed to have caught the contagious happy vibe while displaying a Scooby-Doo-like grin. The energy confirmed there was no trouble. But what would make her daughter act in such a jubilant manner and make such a merry, unannounced visit?

"Wow, baby, he must have been quite impressive!" was Denise's response after sizing up the situation.

With the joy of a child rushing to explain their good fortune, Phoenix nearly shouted, "MAMA Oh my God! He's better than I dreamed he'd be!!"

"Well, damn. Go pour us some wine and I'll be right down to hear all about it."

Phoenix shook her head, 'yes,' and as she made her way to the door, she turned, clasped her hands together, and smiled the widest, most hopeful display of all her teeth. An expression that caused her mother to tease, "Oh my. Does he have an older brother?"

Phoenix laughed and rushed from the room with BooBaby following eagerly behind.

Denise let a long, slow exhale escape before a hopeful smile came across her face. She weighed how well she knew her daughter's dating habits and concluded that if this man made her feel this good before lovemaking, then this is going to be quite an emotional ride.

Sunday, January 12, 2014

DENISE LIVED IN THE INDIAN VILLAGE NEIGHBORHOOD. After Stokely joined Denise and Phoenix at church, she invited him over for dinner. But before dinner, they needed to walk the dog for her daily trek around the community.

"I think my mama likes you," Phoenix shared as she and Stokely walked BooBaby through heavy snow.

Stokely smiled, "I like her. She seems so cool. Has she always been so cool?"

Phoenix laughed, "You know how when girls get in their twenties, they kinda get into a friendship thing with their mothers?" Stokely replied, "Mmm-hmm." Phoenix continued, "That's where we've been for years." Phoenix paused a bit before laughing aloud, "Actually our worst period was when I could start fitting her clothes. I would borrow her stuff - the stuff she barely wore, mind you - and she'd get all mad." Phoenix was cracking up, "Those were our worst times."

"Y'all didn't have issues with boys?"

"You know, considering that I had some faint understanding of why my parents divorced, I just, I don't know, I guess you could say I followed her coaching when it came to boys." Phoenix thought about it some more before adding, "I think I scared off most boys." She laughed. "I mean, even in middle school, I was talking about how the all-girl dance troupe for our school band was an extension of patriarchy - none of the boys was checking for a thirteen-year-old feminist."

They both laughed. Stokely added, "Yeah, you was ahead of your time with that." He laughed a little harder, "I didn't meet any bell hooks disciples until I got to college. You was dropping knowledge early!"

He gave her a fist bump.

"What about you? How did your parents deal with you and teenaged dating?"

Stokely was figuring how to answer without getting into Songhai and her situation. He chose a humorous route, "Well my dad said there are only two kind of women."

Phoenix and BooBaby stopped, "Oh yeah?"

"Yeah."

"And what are they?"

"Oh easy; the woman who will kill you and the woman who will make you kill yourself."

Phoenix laughed so hard that BooBaby began barking.

Stokely was a little confused but laughed along uneasily.

"You know, I don't think I'm ready for those details," Phoenix added between giggles.

"Yeah, I'll have to fill you in later," Stokely said as he turned the conversation another way. "But my mom, she - wait I got to do it like she did me." He stood in front of Phoenix and cradled her face in his palms while impersonating his mother. "Stokely, I know little boys think with their little thing-thing and that gets them in a lotta situations they ain't ready for. So, hear me when I tell you, the easier it is for you to get your little thing-thing in her, the harder it will be to get rid of her. If you're lucky, it'll just be your reputation, but it could be disease or babies from a woman you don't care for."

"Dang, your mom kicked it like that?"

"She kept it one-hundred." Stokely paused, "Well, almost one-hundred."

"What do you mean?"

"Well ... you see, there is nothing little about my thing-thing."

He watched her as the picture came to her mind, then she laughed and started hitting him, "Stokely, you are a fool!!"

BooBaby barked along in merriment.

29

IF IT ISN'T LOVE

New Edition

Wednesday, January 15, 2014

"*C*uddling with clothes," was the description that prompted a chuckle from Stokely.

He was drinking coffee in his apartment after spending the night with Phoenix at her loft. Their date at Baker's Keyboard Lounge was definitely on some *Love Jones* shit but Stokely enjoyed every minute of it.

The band, *Nzinga*, did a heartwarming tribute to Angela Bofill while Phoenix mulled over a brief phone conversation with her estranged father. On one hand, Stokely's growing attachment fueled a desire to do something, say something, or fix the something regarding her sadness about her father. On the other hand, as his father had repeatedly told him, there is a wisdom that comes with thoughtful restraint. Last night was his effort at thoughtful restraint and it ended up with him sharing the bed with a woman he could see himself loving for years to come. Moreover, restraint allowed him the space to really see and hear her. The more he watched, the more beautiful she became. As a connoisseur of feminine beauty, he was accustomed to the woman whose beauty is so striking that during the first meeting, it is as if one is punched in face by the intense strikingness of her beauty. However, the more she is seen, the less striking the beauty is and the more familiar it becomes.

Phoenix was a whole 'nuther thing. Indeed, she was beautiful during that first meeting, but it was as if her physical and spiritual beauty coalesced and subtly increased with each passing moment. It was as if her lips were fuller, her smile brighter, and her eyes were more alluring. Considering the morose undertone of her conversation, Ray Charles could see that she was not trying to seduce Stokely; however, her vulnerability intensified her beauty and in turn increased his compulsion to hold and protect her. When it came to romantic relationships, Stokely was no beginner; but the feelings that were growing towards Phoenix held him captive in a way he had never experienced.

His father told him about the "high" that comes with really paying attention to a woman and how what is seen triggers internal emotion. Cleve certainly shared a treasure chest of truth with that lesson.

Wednesday, July 26, 1967

THE MORNING SUNLIGHT SHAPED AN ALLURING OUTLINE OF Elaine's body as she slept following a tumultuous day of activity.

Cleve was awake. Sitting with his back to the wall, simultaneously admiring the view and replaying the events of the last twenty four hours. Shit was popping off all around in his neighborhood and he intended to skip town for a few days until things calmed. He hadn't thought farther than heading to Flint. He had no way of knowing he'd meet Elaine.

"Meeting her" is a misnomer. Never in his wildest dreams would he have imagined meeting a lady in the way he met Elaine. But, the truth was that amid a cacophony of chaos, he was introduced to a lovely young lady who, despite all his cool urgings, made his heart flutter.

Just as it was fluttering as his eyes traced that wonderfully enticing curve from her hip down to her stomach and up to her shoulder. Considering the instability she described as her life, he wanted to provide as much peace as she would allow him to share. He knew talking about how what he would do paled in comparison to doing it, so if he wanted her to have peace and stability, he was just going to have to be it. Should she choose to be with him, she damn sure would never doubt making the best choice.

Wednesday, January 15, 2014

THE FIRST THING STOKELY NOTICED UPON ARRIVING IN HIS office was the message taped to his computer screen in his officemate's jumbled penmanship. He chuckled to himself while recalling that his officemate is a retired architect, a creator of designs with precision; yet, he wrote with a carelessness that seemed to imply he was saving his precision for something more important.

The message was for Stokely to call Attorney Mankiller.

Without delay, his thumb pressed the number into his cell phone and awaited her pick-up.

After the third ring, she answered, "Laverne Mankiller, here. How can I help you?"

"Attorney Mankiller, this is Stokely Robeson. I got the message to give you a call."

"Yes, Stokely! I'm glad you called. Please pardon my hurriedness, but I'm in between meetings."

"Oh, okay. Should I call back?"

"Better than that. I have two things I need for you to do." She did not wait for his consent because she already knew he was onboard. "First, join me at the Huron Correctional Facility on Wednesday, January 29th at 9:00 am for a parole hearing for Songhai and second, do not tell anyone, especially your parents. Let's only inform them should we get a favorable outcome."

Despite the previous disappointments that accompanied Song's denied parole appeals, the new hope for his sister's return home trumped past disappointment and that hope's enthusiasm was evident in his response, "Yes! And Yes!"

"Good. Okay Stokely, I have to run. I'll see you soon."

"Alright and thank you, Attorney Mankiller. Thanks a million!"

"My pleasure Stokely. Okay. Take care."

Stokely was still holding his phone and smiling with ambitious hope long after Attorney Mankiller had hung up.

30

IF YOU THINK YOU'RE LONELY NOW

Bobby Womack

Saturday, January 18, 2014

*I*f Stokely channeled Florida Evans from *Good Times* and yelled, "Damn, Damn, DAMN!"; it would not capture the profound confusion that followed what should have been a beautifully romantic night.

As he slumped against the wall in the lobby of Lafayette Tower West awaiting the elevator. He recalled the joy shared between him and Phoenix as they perused the displays at the black tie event that is the North American Auto Show Charity Gala. Things were blissfully romantic until they met Tanya and her husband, Oscar. Oscar is a board member of the agency for which Stokely has just begun working and most importantly, he was Phoenix's estranged father.

Stokely recalled the collective shock which caused what appeared to be Oscar's heart attack. He recalled doing CPR on Oscar - which, what the fuck? Resuscitating your ex-girlfriend's husband has got to be some of the most ironic shit ever.

The elevator door opened and after Stokely stepped in,

the closing of the doors replicated the feelings of being closed-in by shit that wasn't his fault. Where did Phoenix go and why did she leave?

He held her coat in his arms since she abandoned it at coat check. She had to be pretty fucking distraught to leave the Auto Show coatless during a frigid Detroit winter night.

As he walked down the hallway toward the apartment he once shared with Tanya, he was overwhelmed with melancholy. He could understand losing Tanya, it was inevitable. But Phoenix too?

He unlocked the door an entered a dark apartment, a darkness that matched his mood. While using his foot to close the door behind him, he failed to lock it. He marched toward the uncomfortable futon in what had been the study room when he and Tanya shared the bedroom. Since she left and took most of the furniture, the thin futon mattress had become a nightly reminder of his life's discomfort.

He balled Phoenix's coat into a pillow and laid his head on it. Her perfume lingered and simultaneously stoked his disappointment and stirred his heartstrings. The confluence of emotions lumped together in his throat and kindled his tear ducts. He pressed his face hard into Phoenix's coat to hold back the tears.

"DAMN, Damn, damn ..."

31

IS MY LIVING IN VAIN?

The Clark Sisters

Tuesday, January 21, 2014

*E*laine was ready. She was not nervous, scared, or anxious. She was ready. Mentally, she was in a *bring-it-on-muthafucka* space.

Too often, the accused do not get an opportunity to share their piece, their perspective, their truth.

Elaine was prepared to share her truth.

Board Member Sharif started the questioning, "Sister Robeson, how do you justify betraying the trust of the community?" Attorney Mankiller stood to shout, "Objection!" but, Elaine held up her hand and shared an expression that said, "I got this."

"I was entrusted to make choices that would benefit the children of Ella Baker Academy. Hiring an additional teacher to decrease class size, establishing a tutorial program, and feeding the children do not strike me as betrayal of the community. Those choices were made for the benefit of the children. Can you show me where the community was betrayed?"

Sharif retreated with what some heard as a whimpering of a retort, "We are asking the questions here."

Board Member Thomas jumped into the fray, "You state your choices as if they were of noble intent while ignoring your contribution to the digital divide." It was a loaded question masquerading as a profound statement. It contained trigger words that made politicians appear to know what they were talking about. Principal Robeson did not need to appear to know what she was talking about, she did in fact truly know her stuff.

"Do you recall my objection during a previous budget meeting?" Elaine asked.

"As my fellow board member has told you, we are asking the questions tonight," Thomas quipped.

"Fine, I will explain that objection." Elaine turned her attention to the audience. "Your school board passed a budget that included a three-quarter time teacher." She looked to the board expecting a response. When they nodded, she continued. "That 30-hour a week teacher is both the librarian in our understocked library and computer teacher. Which means she teaches in the library one week and the computer room the next. Keep in mind, that she works from 8:00 am to 2:00pm and her duties include time monitoring the cafeteria"

She paused to make certain that she was being followed before continuing, "Within a month, an Ella Baker Academy student would spend a little less than two hours in the computer lab. Those state-of-the-art computers and their accompanying software packages and licensing and training ..." Elaine said those things while extending individual fingers on her left hand and bending them back with her right hand. "That you all agreed to purchase would be underutilized, and thus the return on that investment pales in comparison to the students' immediate needs."

To drive home her point, she added, "Real educators know, technology, no matter how shiny and new, is just a tool; it does not replace quality instruction from a caring teacher. Keep that in mind when you allocate money ..." Elaine lifted open palms to mimic a weighing scale, "Fancy technology is instant gratification with short-term results and quality instruction is a sure investment with long-term results."

There was silence as everyone processed Elaine's point. She went on to explain, "While those computers would look great for photo-ops and cash from the sale would have bene-fited your friends at the computer company, as a steward of the community, I acted upon what would be of greater benefit to the students ..." She did the individual extended finger point and press with opposing hand thing again, "Hire an additional teacher to decrease class size, establish a tuto-rial program, and feed the children."

Board chair Van Vetchen blurted angrily while pointing an accusatory finger, "YOU work for us! You do not have the authority to arbitrarily chose what is best for the children. That is our job!"

Elaine folded her arms and leaned back in her chair. Her incredulous expression could have been read to say, "This bitch done lost her everlasting mind..." Her verbal response was stated with professional coldness, "I work for the chil-dren and families of Ella Baker Academy." Then she leaned forward and added rhetorically, "The hardest thing about leading a school, is that everyone thinks they know how to do your job." She raised both palms to the sky and hunched her shoulders when she said, "Why?" it was on cue with the thoughts of nearly all the audience members. "Because they attended school," she leaned back and re-folded her arms with a matter-of-fact smirk.

Cleve and Stokely shared knowing glances. They knew the

Elaine on the stand was a lioness who had held her peace, too long.

Before Reverend Thigpen could share his bombast, Elaine pointed a sweeping finger at the board, "I have more education degrees, certifications, and training than all of you combined. I have spent more time teaching than all you of combined and squared." Then she added very deliberately, "A lady does not reveal her age; yet, I have been working in schools since Nixon was in the White House and despite all my experience and expertise, you believe that you know student needs better than I do." At this point she interlocked her fingers, crossed one leg over the other, and brought her hands to rest upon her knee. "Now tell me, how can that be?"

The audience waited for one of the board members to say that they were asking the questions. None of them did. Board member McLeod broke the silence with an attempt to steer the session to more civil grounds. She recognized Elaine's truth, but wanted to fulfill her duty as a board member. "Principal Robeson, during the time your plan was in place, what outcomes did you see?"

Through telepathy, Elaine communicated a 'Thank you' to McLeod as she replied, "There is a popular adage that students 'don't care how much you know until they know how much you care' - when we feed students, they are affirmed in how much we care. I am also convinced that the correlation between the remarkable uptick in our assessment performance is due to the extra teacher and tutorial program." She paused to let the concepts sink-in.

Reverend Thigpen was stirring and visibly uncomfortable as if he were going to explode, a moment which granted McLeod one more question. "I want to be clear, my issue is not with the outcome nor the rationale. Principal Robeson, I take issue with the fact that you willingly kept the school board in the dark. Did your doubt in us cause you to make the choices that led to these hearings?"

"I appreciate your candor. Indeed my experiences with this board fueled my doubt in your ability to follow my rationale. This board has members who are genuine in their concern as well as opportunists seeking Clintonesque avenues to bolster their public personas." The Clintonesque comment was directed at Van Vetchen and Thomas, both of whom were in Elaine's realm of vision when she spoke. "Frankly Mrs. McLeod, considering what was at stake, I just believe that some things were better left unsaid."

When Thigpen slammed his hand, he stunned everyone in attendance. "As God is my witness, we will not entertain anymore of your slander in this forum," as he rose from his seat. He thundered from dais and took center stage like a bull-headed cross examiner.

Attorney Mankiller rose from her seat to stand between her client and the accuser. The hearing was transforming into a spectacle.

Thigpen jabbed his finger in the air with each accusation.

"We did you a favor by hiring you when you weren't even good enough for DPS!"

He stepped closer.

"We put up with your deceit as you led my school away from the Lord's path!"

He took another step.

"We endured your highfaluting haughtiness despite your mediocre leadership!"

The next finger jab was from Mankiller, whom in his anger, Thigpen did not even see.

She jabbed her finger in his shoulder and honed her unintimidated gaze directly into his eyes, "Reverend Thigpen, you are out of line."

He pushed the attorney.

Cleve, Stokely, and Brother Sharif bolted from their seats.

Andrette hollered, "Oh hell nawl!"

Sharif grabbed Thigpen and Cleve wrapped his arms around Elaine. Stokely assumed a referee's stance as if beckoning boxers to return to their corners.

Van Vetchen finally began pounding the gavel.

Mankiller's request for a recess was accepted.

NEARLY A HALF HOUR LATER, THE HEARING RESUMED WITH Thigpen's question, "Why should we trust you?"

Everyone leaned forward.

"The students," Elaine paused. "Trust me."

"The parents," she took a deep breath. "Trust me."

"The teachers and staff, they trust me."

"I believe that some of you", she pointed in the direction of the school board, "trust me."

"But Reverend Thigpen, the main source of distrust stems from you." Everyone gasped at the obvious truth. "As an alleged man of God, you have made my tenure at Ella Baker, pure hell." Eyes widened around the room at Elaine's declaration.

"For too long, I ... we've allowed your boisterousness to bully us; but now Reverend, it's my time." She took a longer, deeper breath before continuing, "All of the years have come to this. All the lesson plans, evaluations, conferences with parents, it has all come to this, being crucified like some criminal." A lump emerged in Elaine's throat, "From the day I read about the accusations in the newspaper until now, this whole spectacle makes me feel ..." a sniffle escaped. "That my work was in vain." Elaine hung her head.

Cleve squeezed back his tears.

Stokely slumped down in his chair.

Attorney Mankiller approached the board and handed each member an envelope. "Inside you will find the terms of agreement for Principal Robeson's resignation ..."

32

TRY A LITTLE TENDERNESS

Otis Redding

Tuesday, January 21, 2014

When they entered their home after the last board meeting, Cleve darted ahead to pour his wife a shot of Martell. Once she downed the drink in one gulp, he escorted her to the living room, where she sat on the sofa. There, he removed her shoes and got another shot. This time, Elaine sipped slowly while Cleve escaped to run a hot bath.

As a plumber, Cleve took great pride in the plumbing work in his home. On this night, he ran hot water in the free standing whirlpool bathtub and dropped a lavender bath bomb in it. He then fumbled around before finding three candles which he lit and placed strategically near the tub.

When he returned to the living room, Elaine had finished the second cognac. He thought, "Two shots downed in less than five minutes? Yep, it's been a long night."

He leaned over, kissed her on her forehead and removed the earrings from each ear. While leaning over, he reached behind her head and unclasped her pearls. He shared a quick thank you prayer as he noted Elaine's short cropped style would not require any type of preparation from him.

He got down on his knees and lovingly removed her watch, rings, and bracelets and sat them on the end table next to her earrings, pearls, and the empty shot glass. He then pulled her to her feet and unbuttoned her blouse.

Forty plus years of marriage had taught Elaine to go with flow when Cleve was in caretaker mode. As a younger woman, she would have asked what he was doing; but as a wiser woman, she knew better than to disturb a man focused on her care.

Knowing how much she cherished her St. John suits, he removed the jacket and folded it neatly over the nearby recliner. He reached behind her, undid the clasp, pulled down the back zipper, and commenced to pulling down her skirt as she balanced herself by holding his shoulders. He folded the skirt neatly and placed it in the recliner chair. He kneeled and pulled down her panty hose and underwear as she again balanced herself with his shoulders as she stepped out of the undergarments. He tugged at the sleeve of blouse, pulled one arm free before the other. The years of familiarity did not the diminish the excitement that accompanied viewing his wife's nakedness. Cleve was usually a cool cat, but he felt his heart began to race and his penis begin to stir.

He reached around her back and undid her bra. When she extended her arms so that he can pull the bra straps from her shoulders, she knew to wrap her arms around his neck. Once he tossed the bra, he lifted his wife and carried her to the bathroom. He said another quick prayer that nothing in his body would give as he lowered his wife into the rising, steaming waters. His prayers were answered and his timing was impeccable as Elaine likes to enter the tub when it's three-quarters full. As she leaned back and sunk into the waters, Cleve retreated for a pair of shot glasses and the Martell, so that they could enjoy their drinks together.

BY THE TIME HE CHANGED INTO HIS LOUNGEWEAR AND joined Elaine in the bathroom, she had the whirlpool jets humming on low.

"Do you think I made a mistake?" Elaine asked as he poured their drinks.

Cleve let out a long sigh, passed her a glass before taking a seat on the floor next to the tub.

"Depends..." he took a sip. "It's not a mistake if this leads to reinvention."

He swirled the drink around before resuming, "But, if you're quitting because you can't take the heat; well, 'Laine, I don't think you're a quitter, so ..." he took another sip.

"That's fair," she said as she slid lower into the tub so the jets could whoosh water into her lower back and the soles of her feet. "It is reinvention, except I don't know what I'm turning into or really what I want to do next."

They sat quietly for a few minutes.

Cleve broke the silence, "I think you need to mentor. Like, what the kids say, yeah, 'you an OG' now. An elder, it's time to get an up-and-coming educator or community servant under your wings and teach them the ropes."

Elaine immediately connected Cleve's idea with Joyce's invitation. "You know I'm going to visit Joyce's school on Thursday. She says she got a presentation for a program for girls that she would like me to work with."

"I thought you said you didn't know what you were doing next," Cleve chuckled.

"I don't. This just a little something for my friend and to pass the time, you know. It's not permanent."

"Mmmmm hhhmmm. How is Joyce doing anyway?"

"I guess she's fine. You know we're coming up on eight years since Earl passed. For a while she wrestled with guilt about care taking of him, but over time and with therapy, she's kinda forgiven herself. I suppose that's part of grief, you know, blaming yourself or second guessing what you could've done or should've done."

"Yeah, that's what they say." Cleve paused for sip then resumed, "You know even though all of us was helping you through, I gotta ask, that Francine ... is she okay?"

"I suppose so, why do you ask?"

"I mean she always been extra, but it seem like she's done got extra extra, you know what I mean?"

"Well, that foolishness with the school board had me so caught up in my own worries that I hadn't noticed. But in the past, when she gets that way, she's overcompensating for something. Trying to act like everything is alright; you know, covering up something."

"I see. When you get a chance, y'all might need to do that sisters' intervention on ya' girl. I don't know what it is but ... I don't know, y'all check it out now, for real."

"Ok baby. It's my turn to return the support, hunh?"

Cleve didn't answer. They sat quietly for a few moments before Elaine asked, "When is Stokely going to tell me what happened?"

Cleve laughed, "That boy know he can fall in love faster than Pepé Le Pew."

They both laughed before Cleve added, "I told him stop by in the morning now that these hearings is behind ya'. I said it wasn't no way I could retell his story straight and answer all yo' questions."

Elaine splashed a little water at him.

"Hey now! My old lady got me these PJs; don't you go gettin' 'em all wet."

"Your old lady?" Elaine remarked sarcastically as she stood

in all her naked sudsy splendor. She drew a gasp of admiration from Cleve who tried to cover it up and play cool. Deep down, that gasp was priceless. She had heard about marriages that lose their spark, to her, Cleve's gasp was proof that she still, they still had that spark. She bent over and playfully balled his collar in her fist to get him to stand. When he stood, she placed both wet palms on chest and leaned in to kiss him.

"Will yo' old lady get mad if I give you a little something something?"

Cleve played along, "She say she don't mind if I play, you know, just as long as I'm home when the street lights come on."

"Well, she's going to be mad because you'll be late tonight."

"Oh, I'm sure she'll be alright."

"I know she will ..."

The kissing intensified.

33

THE THRILL IS GONE

B.B. King

Wednesday, January 22, 2014

Following every mountaintop summit comes the necessary descent down the mountainside. Mountain climbers would confirm that the descent is significantly harder than the ascent.

Numerous factors contribute to the increased demands of the descent; yet, a few stand out more than others. During the climb-up, there is the freshness that comes with the beginning of a task. Consider running a race of multiple laps around the track, the first lap is a breeze because all the hope and energy is high. However, the toll of multiple laps or for the climber, the demands of hours climbing, drains the energy.

Unlike the runner, the summiting of the mountain is the dessert during the middle of the meal. The exuberant joy and accompanying thrills are experienced in the middle of the work. Novices become distracted by that accomplishment and minimize the more tedious work that comes with descending the mountain.

. . .

ELLA BAKER ACADEMY HAD A MOUNTAINTOP MOMENT
when they were designated as a Blue Ribbon School. Under
the leadership of Principal Robeson, they had become the
most remarkable charter school success story in the state.
Moreover, the camaraderie built within the staff during the
preceding years had Baker Academy running like a well-oiled
machine.

Baker Academy continued humming forward like a car on
cruise control during the first half of the 2013-2014 school
year. They watched in horror as their leader was lied on,
cheated, talked about, and mistreated. However, their synergy
kept the day-to-day operations of the school going as if Principal Robeson were still at work.

But, she wasn't.

And word has it, that she never will again.

For the mountain climber, the first few steps following
the summit are carried by the lingering sense of accomplishment. The first few months after the Blue Ribbon designa-
tion was comparable to those post-summit steps for the
Baker staff. Yet, there comes a moment during the descent
when shit get real. When the climber notices the darkening
of the day, their own diminished energy, and the decrease in
their supplies. That moment of descent became real to Baker
Academy staff when they received messages via the emergency chain of communication - the phone communication
they used when sharing school would be closed - to be at a
mandatory staff meeting at 6:00 am on Wednesday morning.

The announcement was made by their new interim leader,
Reverend Amos Thigpen.

THE UPHEAVAL THE SHORT NOTICE OF THE ANNOUNCEMENT caused in the life of the staff was an indicator of things to come. Somehow teachers had to make unusual arrangements for getting their own kids to school. Morning routines were upturned and fear and irritation were mounting.

At no time ever had Principal Robeson said a meeting was mandatory. She didn't have to. She did not conduct meetings for meeting's sake and she did not lead through fear and intimidation.

Most importantly, her scheduled staff meetings had refreshments.

Reverend Thigpen was not that thoughtful.

He stood at the front office door with his arms folded and a scowl on his face. He did not have the foresight to at least hold the meeting in a place where the staff could take a seat.

"Y'alls' principal quit on y'all," was his declaration to start the meeting.

A number of the staff were present at the hearing and knew Principal Robeson had resigned. They all incorrectly assumed that since they had been maintaining the school so well, that this day would go like the previous ones.

The late night call challenged that and this harangue by Reverend Thigpen confirmed that Ella Baker Academy was about to decline.

The lobby of Baker Academy held all the staff. The handful who were late - not because they were irresponsible, but the abruptness of this meeting usurped their routines - were dressed down by the reverend.

"You call yourself committed to the Lord's work coming late to a mandatory meeting?" When they attempted to reply, "The Lord is not pleased with your casualness toward his work," was his shout-down tactic to keep them from responding.

Then what was possibly an aside between Thigpen and

the Lord, he said in a lower tone, "Father forgive them for they know not what they do."

For thirty minutes as the staff stood with their coats on and bags in their hands, Reverend Thigpen proceeded to rant about how things were going to change and how they needed to get their act together or find another place to work. He pushed his dagger of shame deeper into the staffs' heart by repeatedly saying, "Not everyone has the anointing to do the Lord's work."

Confusion, anger, and irritation were the most common feelings among the staff. Half of whom had only known the benevolent leadership of Principal Robeson and found Thigpen's dictatorial address condescending and dispiriting.

Reverend Thigpen did not open the floor for questions. He simply clapped his hands twice and told the staff they were dismissed. He then turned into the office and slammed the door.

The Ella Baker Academy staff looked at each other in disbelief. What had previously been a great place to work had been subjected to a cloud of evil calling itself the Lord's work. The younger staff recalled Scar taking over Pride Rock in *The Lion King*. The more seasoned staff recalled when the state took over Detroit Public Schools. All the staff knew the truth, the thrill of working at Ella Baker Academy was gone.

34

ONLY THE STRONG SURVIVE

Jerry Butler

Wednesday, January 22, 2014

*T*he folded suit on the recliner and the bra hanging from the lampshade said different things about one truth: Stokely's parents still had their mojo working. As he made his way to the back room where his mother goes for reflection and tranquility, he smelled the coffee that had been brewed, observed the dishes in the sink, and even noted the remaining bacon on the stove. After helping himself to one of the remaining strips of bacon, he figured Cleve and Elaine shared a night of lovemaking and a morning of breakfast chatter. All of those observations became mental notes or more accurately, relationship goals for Stokely. His parents proved that a healthy love life wasn't just for the young. He was smiling at that thought as he entered his mother's room.

"Well, look who's here, Mr. Love 'Em and Leave 'Em!" Elaine shared with a mirth Stokely hadn't heard in several months.

"Aw Ma, maybe you should call me, Mr. Love 'Em and Get Left," he replied half-jokingly as he hugged his mother and kissed her on the cheek. Elaine laughed heartily at her son's self-depreciation as she patted the spot next to her on the love seat.

"When your daddy came home the other day from helping you move, he summed it up like this ..." she sort of straightened herself and brought her fingertips together like yogis before they say 'mmmmmm.' She then mocked Cleve's Eddie Levert sounding baritone and said, "That boy done lost two good women in two weeks, that ought be a record!" while holding up two fingers and then flipping them from the back-hand side to correspond with the two women, two weeks point-of-emphasis.

Stokely shook his head in embarrassed amusement. "Ma, if someone would have told me that, I wouldn't have believed them. But ..." he allowed a long defeated sigh as his mother patted him on his back, "I lived it so I know it's true."

After a moment of silence to mourn lost loves, Elaine channeled a patient maternal therapist voice and said, "Let's take a little time to look at what happened." She paused as she stopped rubbing his back and reached for his hand with which she intertwined her fingers. "We can look at it, unpack it, sort it out, and make sense of what you need to learn, what you need to change, and what you need to leave alone. Let's start with Tanya." At this point, she placed her finger under his chin and turned his head so that he was facing her.

"Falling in love with a married woman Stokely, you did know that was precarious from the start, right?"

"Yyeeaaaahhh," he almost whispered in a defeated tone.

"But, let's look at it a different way, without the guilt. Tell me, what you saw in her. You know, the magic that made you feel you wanted to start something with her."

Stokely's face brightened. "Tanya is beautiful. Like she is like, majestic with it. Have you ever seen her walk into a room? Mama, damn, it's more than her physical beauty and curves. She got this thing, that, that ..."

"Let's call that presence."

"Yeah, presence with like, some vibe radiating off of it."

Elaine chuckled at Stokely's descriptions, his facial expressions, and the knowledge that he was definitely in love.

"Stokely, I think you have a thing, or let's say an appreciation for certain things that you express with admiration. Tanya's presence and vibe trigger things in everyone. I'm sure some people probably mistake her for being aloof or, what they probably say is 'she think she all that,' but, really they are responding to her presence with their insecurities."

Stokely shook his head in agreement.

Elaine continued, "Considering that you are Cleveland Robeson's son, you aren't intimidated or discouraged by that type of presence in a woman. Now I'm going to tell you this and while I can't speak for Tanya, I would bet I'm close to her truth." Stokely looked at his mother with an open receptiveness to receive what she was going to share. "Women get hit on or flirted with numerous times, but most boys - 'cause a real man doesn't do this - boys try to contain a woman's magic. Possess it. Sort of box it up as theirs. A grown woman who is no longer impressed with attention, but really prefers something meaningful, she is past that bullstuff. So your ability to love her and allow her to be - that's the thing that connected her to you. I'd bet my entire savings on that."

Stokely was a little confused. Elaine went on, "Me and your daddy been together since '67. At first, his handsomeness and caring spirit attracted me. Then as we grew together, his support and consistency kept us together." She patted Stokely's leg, "As a girl who spent her childhood shuffled from this house to the next, and this distant relative to the next, the stability Cleve's consistency provides is what makes me fall in love with him over and over again." Stokely smiled as the description his mother shared of his father fit the image of the man he admired. "Now I'm going to go back to possession. Cleve and I, we are together. One plus one - so we're twice as good."

Stokely jokingly added, "You know Michael Jackson sang that thing about love not being a possession."

Elaine laughed. Although she didn't know the Michael Jackson song, she knew that if Stokely was making connections with what she was saying to something else, that meant he was really hearing her. Yet, the fact that he connected it to a song conjured the memories of him spending his last money on records, cassettes, and CDs. The irritants caused by children sometimes transform into warm memories of their peculiarities.

"So Michael sang about what made you and Tanya work, and since we know that she was married, and thus had another life to which you were not privy, let's just say it had to end at some point and it did. It appears that you enjoyed yourself." They both laughed at that truth. "Now baby, I ain't going to venture too far into your grown man business, but I'm going to guess that the physical component y'all shared contributed to the length of time y'alls' fling or whatever lasted. With that being the case, a little one for the road or a little something for old time's sake opportunity may arise. If you really going to grow on and heal from the heartbreak, I'm going to suggest you treat that opportunity with a 'thanks but no thanks.'"

Elaine observed her son's head nod and gathered that the opportunity may have already presented itself. Nevertheless, she pressed ahead, "So while you were complicit in that love affair, its ending ain't on you. Let Tanya go." Elaine pursed her lips, furrowed her brow, and tilted her head toward Stokely. He knew to respond, "Yes Ma," to which she smiled.

"Now the new girl, don't say her name, I'mma remember,

uh, uh ..." Elaine was snapping her fingers. The forming of the F sound on Stokely's lips was the last clue Elaine needed, "Phoenix! Yes, Phoenix." Stokely laughed.

"Okay, Cleve told me that the two of you was at the big Auto Show shindig where y'all met Tanya," Elaine made the statement in a tone that asked for confirmation. Stokely nodded 'Yes.'

"And it turns out that Tanya's husband is Phoenix's dad?" Elaine asked that more intently.

Stokely grimaced tightly, "Yeeeaaah."

Elaine smiled and shook her head, "Son, I ain't never, ever heard anything like that. But, it is so like you to be in the unlikeliest of situations." They both laughed at this truth.

"When you showed me her picture the other day when we were talking, you had that proud glow that you just had when describing Tanya, and from that, I know your heart is in the right place. Plus, you've gone to church with the girl and had dinner with her mama, so I know you sho-nuff serious." They shared nods of agreement.

"I'm a little reserved about the one woman to the next thing that this appears to be, but you and I know things ain't always as they appear." It was a throw-away reference to what she had just been through with the school board and Stokely understood. "Cleve also said, when Phoenix realized who and what, she ran away." Stokely smiled as he pictured his father restating the story verbatim.

"Yeah Ma, she took off."

"Before or after you did the CPR on her dad?"

"I'm guessing when I was doing it. Oscar, her dad's name is Oscar, looked like he had a heart attack or something and fell down. I saw Phoenix's reaction to that, but by the time I did the CPR and the paramedics came, she was gone."

Elaine exhaled, "Stokely, son ... this sounds like a Lifetime movie." They laughed again.

"But seriously, as sure as the night follows the day, I'm going tell you that she wasn't running from you." Elaine did that pursed lip, furrowed brow, head tilt thing again. "You were there and your actions contributed to the situation, but her leaving sounds like a whole lot of confusion and emotionality in response to the circumstances," they were both silent for a moment.

"So like your dad told you, I'm going to tell you - Stokely, if you really care for Phoenix the way you are letting on, do not try to make something happen."

Stokely's expression said, 'But Ma' to which Elaine did that pursed lip, furrowed brow, head tilt thing again.

"Give her space and time. If you really care or love her, that is the only way for this thing to work."

Stokely's shoulders slumped in defeat.

Elaine rubbed his back.

"If you force it, you may get a moment, but you'll mess up the long-term. If you give her space and time, you'll miss some moments, but the possibility of something more substantial and enduring will be there."

Much like the expression of reluctant acceptance Stokely had as a seven year-old when Cleve announced, "I took your training wheels off that bike. You either gonna ride or fall but you're done teeter tottering with training wheels." Stokely looked at his mother with an I-don't-see-what-you're-saying-but-I'm-going-to-go-along trust expression of acceptance.

Perhaps he was ready after all.

FOUR WOMEN

Nina Simone

Thursday, January 23, 2014

*J*oyce Keys has been the principal of Tubman Technical Academy for its sixteen-year existence. Two of her most redeeming leadership attributes are her emphatic listening and willingness to adapt. Those attributes are not strategies but genuine extensions of her character. Joyce was the type of person with whom after a five minute discussion, one would feel compelled to share a hug.

Cynthia McNair was a second-year teacher at Tubman. Miss McNair is passionate, idealistic, and an obvious acolyte of Principal Keys. Their relationship is more than just a mentor and mentee, it is akin to that of a mother and daughter. Cynthia was twelve-years-old when Tubman opened, and she started the seventh grade. Then, like now, Principal Keys was her hero.

Elaine Robeson was Principal Keys' best friend. This particular afternoon was her first visit to Tubman since the debacle that ended her last principalship. Joyce considers Elaine's presence an opportunity for her to heal. Elaine is just going along with her friend's urging, unsure of why she is here, and whether she will come back.

Phoenix Ellison leads Building Beautiful Daughters (BBD), a nonprofit that offers programs geared toward the holistic development of young girls. She is at Tubman to convince Principal Keys of the value that BBD would add to the learning community. She is not aware that Principal Keys has already concluded that she would pilot BBD during the second semester of the school year. She is also not aware that Miss McNair's presence is an attempt at orchestrating the future collaboration of two dynamic young women by Principal Keys.

Most of all, she is clueless that the woman who introduced herself as Mrs. Elaine is the mother of the man she was growing to love until the incident. Phoenix has built a mental barrier around the incident and her last time seeing Stokely. In her heart, she wants to see Stokely again. He was just the type of person she could talk to about what she was going through; except, he was all-up-in the circumstances that needed discussing. She wants to pick up where they left off, but right now she is unable to think of him without thinking of the incident. She needs time to clear her head and grow BBD.

"I WISH TO START BY SHARING A HEARTFELT 'THANK YOU' for you taking time to listen to my presentation," Phoenix conveyed gratitude in her eye contact and body language with each of the other three women. Her gratitude was also the flip side of an emotional coin that also contained disappointment. Phoenix still carried the bruise of being abruptly rescinded at the last school to whom she presented BBD. That bruise was evident when she said, "I want to be candid that my services are geared toward girls. I agree our boys would benefit from similar services; yet, my expertise is developing girls."

She paused and looked around.

Joyce smirked confidently, "Honey, you let me take care of the boys. We're listening to you because all of us know that our girls need devoted mentoring into womanhood. So, tell us about how you build them beautifully."

Joyce's comment had the intended effect. Phoenix relaxed and her smile shined a little brighter.

Elaine saw how Phoenix captivated her son. While she was indeed attractive, her essence and her purpose seemed to amplify a more meaningful, spiritual beauty. Moreover, it appeared her self-concept was not based upon how pretty she thought herself to be. This young lady is genuine. She is the real deal.

Cynthia was impressed also. Like committed teachers everywhere, she worried about how her students fared when they left her classroom. In Phoenix, she saw a kindred spirit and an opportunity to extend love and support to students beyond the school day.

The scheduled thirty-minute meeting exceeded ninety minutes. Amid exchanges of good ideas and the drafting of a memorandum of understanding, there was laughter and growing mutual respect. Joyce was affirmed in the value BBD would bring to Tubman. Cynthia was thrilled at the prospect of working with Phoenix. Phoenix was relieved and excited over potentially securing BBD's biggest contract. Elaine pondered upon Cleve's comment about mentoring the next generation and how she would navigate this relationship without revealing her connection to Stokely. Of course, he wasn't mentioned; yet, Elaine correctly imagined that Phoenix's reaction to the Auto Show fiasco was one that required measured recovery time.

36

GUESS WHO I SAW TODAY

Nancy Wilson

Monday, January 27, 2014

*I*n his mind, Wellington Shelby was a cosmopolitan young man. The type of man who made others swoon with his effervescent charm. His propensity for excessive cologne and too-tight tailored suits provided him with a fashionable edge to accentuate his boy-band-lead-singer handsomeness. His hairless face, well-manicured nails, and immaculate diction made him the poster boy for diversity efforts of otherwise conservative, all-White corporations. How could a company be racist when they employed such a talent as Wellington?

Not all were enamored by Wellington, particularly in his new role as the Executive Assistant for the Detroit Public Schools' Emergency Manager. The whole Emergency Manger thing is a very sore spot with many Detroiters, who weren't fond of some appointee from the state capitol telling them what to do. Even if that appointee shared their same skin color.

Nevertheless, the Emergency Manger rode into town on a

white horse named School Reform. He threatened the teacher's union, usurped the democratically elected school board, and riled the public sentiment with evidence of the district's financial inconsistencies. Usually, a glance over his left shoulder would bring Wellington into view. Perpetually tied to multiple smartphones, Wellington conveyed a purposeful hurriedness and an aloof, too-professional polish that garnered consistent side-eyes from those disenchanted with this alleged reform. The elders, who have seen it all, would denounce Wellington as full of himself. Community activists would preface their comments about him with, "Then this pretty-assed negro ..." DPS administrators loathed his appearance because he was the harbinger of forthcoming bad news and bullshit.

THAT IS WHY WHEN FRANCINE HUNG HER COAT IN HER office following school dismissal, she was thoroughly stunned to see Wellington sitting at her desk.

Enraptured in two phones, he did not see the snarl on her face when she initially recognized him.

"Obviously, this is not a social call," Francine stated as a cold greeting.

Wellington stood, tugged at his snug-fitting sport coat, buttoned it, and extended his hand for a shake. "Good afternoon Principal Franklin, it is a pleasure to finally meet."

Francine looked at his hand as if it were a serpent's tongue, then looked at him with an expression of barely concealed suspicion.

It took a few awkward seconds before Wellington realized that she was not going to shake his hand. He attempted to transition by asking, "Would it be a bother if I took a seat?"

"You weren't bothered before so don't get all bothered now," she retorted.

He smiled meekly before sitting.

"I suppose you are contemplating the inspiration for my visit this fine afternoon."

"I wouldn't say it like that. I was thinking more along the lines of 'Why is his ass in my damn office?'"

The meek smile returned.

Francine folded her arms.

"Principal Franklin, our team has been reviewing contracts signed by building administrators," he paused.

Francine's arms remained folded, but she shifted over to the other hip, tilted her head, and raised her eyebrows in a 'Yeah, what?' manner.

This is the only time physically imposing and Wellington Shelby will be in the same sentence as he was anything but that. He was not a large or medium-sized man and nothing about him suggested any type of physicality. So, Francine's imposing posture towering over him as he sat was unsettling and intimidating. He was out of place in this dynamic. He is naturally more of a provocateur who leaves the fighting to the big bully that he represents. He was accustomed to administrators cowering in his presence. His assumptions left him ill-prepared for Francine.

Francine didn't speak. She didn't give in to the defensiveness that others resorted to at this prelude to accusations. She just looked directly at him with a 'What else you got to say' affect.

"Our review prompted some questions that we figured you are the most qualified to answer."

"Actually, my lawyer is even more qualified than I am to answer your questions."

Wellington allowed a phony laugh to escape and mask his growing discomfort. "Oh no, no Principal Franklin. Who needs attorneys when sharing truths among friends?"

"Friends?" She said it with a tone more repulsive than molded tuna.

At that moment, Wellington began imagining how he would leave. "Perhaps a visit downtown would be more comfortable for you to talk."

Francine jumped right in, "Or maybe it would be more comfortable for you with your team around?" She allowed the sarcasm and implications of his fear to hang in the air for a moment. Then resumed, "Mr. Shelby, your visits are infamous, and your visit here today screams 'BULLSHIT LIES AHEAD!'"

The raising of her voice startled him as he jumped from his seat.

Francine laughed a mocking laugh. "Yeah, we better take this meeting downtown with my attorney because you don't want it with me, you fake-ass scallawag."

As he retreated from his authoritative disposition, Wellington's confidence was shook. He now knew that there was no place for halfway intimidators in Principal Franklin's office.

Principal Franklin also knew something - the thread of her pilfering practices was exposed and would soon unravel. Tough talk aside, her worse fears began to bubble inside like the onset of diarrhea.

37

WE'RE BLESSED

Fred Hammond & Radical for Christ

Wednesday, January 29, 2014

*A*s a teenager, Songhai Robeson eschewed fake nails. She preferred clear polish on her smoothly trimmed and rounded natural nails. At the time, it was a small expression of the value of natural beauty - a value she adopted from her mother, Elaine. Teenaged Songhai would have been repulsed at the chewed nubs of nails worn by the prison-weary adult Songhai. Teenaged Songhai would have been additionally repulsed at the circumstances that led to adult Songhai serving nearly twenty years in prison. It has been years since adult Songhai had been able to connect with the spring of optimistic hope that coursed through the spirit of teenaged Songhai. The oppressiveness of prison has nearly smothered all of her youthful optimism.

The spring of optimism had been reduced to a trickle, a small pulse of hope supplied by the incessant advocacy of her family.

When her little brother, Stokely, entered the chambers

with the new attorney, Laverne Mankiller, a slight surge of hope made its way through the trickle of optimism that remained. Songhai had steadfastly avoided hope while longing for a reason to hope again. Would today be the day?

"YOUR HONOR, WE ARE REQUESTING AN IMMEDIATE PAROLE for Miss Songhai Robeson. She has served nearly all of the sentence imposed upon an immature, love-struck teenager. During her years served, even the murderer she accompanied has been granted parole," Attorney Mankiller paused and swallowed back the bile of disgust she felt toward the disproportionate sentencing of women of color before resuming. "Let's imagine, a high school girl driving her boyfriend to the store. She was unaware of the scuffle and disagreements that go on inside the store. The court records show that the visit to the store was not a robbery, but an altercation rooted in someone looking at the murderer 'wrong.' Miss Robeson has been designated an accomplice to murder for the crime of driving her boyfriend, of whom she was unaware was in possession of a gun and doubly unaware of his having been involved in a shooting she did not witness. Your honor, she simply drove the car in which he was riding."

Mankiller allowed that truth to linger.

"Nearly twenty years later, we wish to acknowledge her time served for that decision and arrive at new decision that would allow her to piece her life back together. Some feel justice was served in her original sentencing; however, no one would feel that there is justice being served in her remaining in prison after the murderer himself has been paroled. Your honor, there is no justice in that fact."

THIS WAS STOKELY'S FIRST PAROLE HEARING WITH HIS

sister and he would not be able to fathom how much hooking his pinky finger with hers despite her handcuffs steadied her confidence. Previous hearings had been attended by their parents, who supported arguments presented by Songhai. This was also Attorney Mankiller's first parole hearing with Songhai. Gamblers would call it luck and church folks would call it a blessing. Whatever one would call it, the strategy of professional representation was a difference maker. Although the outcome of the hearing came late in the midnight hour of Song's prison sentence, God definitely turned it around.

Songhai Robeson would be paroled Wednesday, February 19, 2014.

———

PRISON HAS A WAY OF STRIPPING ONE TO THEIR CORE. TIME stretches nearly infinitely while hope compresses significantly. The passing of each day provided Songhai a bit more toughened skin, heightened aggression, and acute protectiveness. However, unlike all the previous days and despite her intimacy with gloom - this night, Song allowed herself hope. While laying in her bunk, she remembered an adage that her mother would share during visits, "Two women looked out from prison bars; one saw the mud and the other saw stars."

The adage was like a business card. Something Song received and put away in a mental pocket of things not frequently used.

However, on this night, she extracted the adage from her memory, followed her mother's wisdom, and chose to see the stars. Despite regret looming monstrously large in one corner of her mind and fear menacingly mounted in another; Song steeled her resolve and with renewed hope, focused on the stars.

The prospect of new life beyond the bars caused Song to

shed silent tears of joy. She foresaw a life to live freely ... under the light of the stars.

38

HE'S MISTRA KNOW-IT-ALL

Stevie Wonder

Thursday, February 6, 2014

It took two weeks for the Ella Baker Academy School Board to call an emergency closed session board meeting. The meeting began at noon at an empty Baker Academy.

Why would a school be empty on an otherwise typical school day?

On the second day of his interim leadership, Reverend Thigpen fired the lead teacher. Four days later, he fired another teacher. He felt justified as he emphasized the *at-will employee* clause in their contracts. However, all could see that he was intentionally ridding the school of Principal Robeson sympathizers and other would-be-objectors to his tyranny.

But not even his perverted gospel could have prepared him for what he faced on the morning of February 6th.

He arrived to discover an empty parking lot and a dark building. There was a lone figure leaning against the front door an hour before school was to begin. It was Andrette

Thomas, the person who was next on Reverend's not-so-secret hit list.

Andrette was loudly chewing her gum when Thigpen approached in a huff. He did not consider saying, 'Good morning.'

"Where is everyone?!" he thundered.

"Oh, you talking to me now?"

"You heard me - where are the teachers?!"

Andrette laughed mockingly as she lifted her hands in a Vanna White manner, "Well, obviously they ain't here."

Reverend stepped into Andrette's personal space. "Listen you got-damn fag, where in the hell is everybody? Hunh? Tell me before I…"

"Before you what? Anoint me with oil and give me a holy ass-whipping? That's what you gonna do REV-er-END?"

Thigpen was getting angrier. Andrette was not intimidated. She continued, "For the record, I am trans. Only ignorant people call other humans 'fags.'"

Thigpen was getting even more heated and was seconds away from blowing his top.

"Did the lawd eva' tell ya that communication is a two way thing?"

Now confusion mixed with Thigpen's growing anger.

"If you knew how to communicate, then your holy ass would have known that everyone called-in sick today." Andrette smirked matter-of-factly. "Looks like you got the school just the way you want it - to yo' damn self!"

With that, Andrette shoved by Reverend and made her way to the bus stop.

"YOU'RE FIRED!" was all that Reverend could say to save face.

Andrette flipped a middle finger in his direction as she walked away. She volunteered for this opportunity to greet

Reverend and the delight it provided was greater than the inconvenience of catching the bus.

As she rounded the corner of the cross street, the first parent for before-school, early-drop-off period arrived. The parents had not been notified of the sick-out protest. They were planning to drop their kids off like any other day. Reverend Thigpen was left to be the dunce who had to explain that school was closed to each car that arrived and each student who walked to school. Quite a few parents shared colorfully profane diatribes as to how Principal Robeson would never do anything like this. Moreover, he could not confidently answer when classes would resume.

Reverend Thigpen endured verbal lashings from 7:00 am until nearly 9:30 am as there was no one to place the automated calls or send mass emails. In his two weeks of leadership, he emphatically reminded staff that the Lord sent him to redeem the school. On this morning, he was going to need the Lord to work in a mighty mysterious way to keep the parents from kicking his ass.

BOARD MEMBER SHARIF DID NOT HOLD BACK, "REVEREND Thigpen you said you got this. You said running a school wasn't no different than running a church! You said you was going to redeem the school, Rev. You said that shit. Now we ain't got no kids and no teachers? What the fuck Rev?!"

While each of the board members would have asked the same question in their own way, none spoke up to address Sharif about his tone and language. They were all too embarrassed at the spectacle that the school was becoming.

Board member Thomas broke the silence, "Surely there is an explanation for all this. Reverend, have you spoken to any of the staff?"

"Besides the damn cafeteria manager, I haven't talked any of those back-stabbing ingrates. After I called you all, I read my bible and consulted with my Lord for guidance in these extreme times."

Board member Van Vetchen was diplomatic in asking, "What did the Lord tell you?"

Sharif shouted in angered sarcasm, "Gettest thou off thy holy pedestal and getteth the damn kids back in school!"

"You will not mock me and my savior!"

Both men stood in a clash of egos that would have taken the form of rams butting horns until Board member McLeod declared, "Gentleman, all that anger will not get our staff and students back."

That truth was a splash of cold water on everyone.

"Reverend. You, me, we, us - we made a mistake," McLeod said softly. The men sat slowly.

"We truly underestimated what Principal Robeson meant to this school."

"The Lord told me to stay the course!"

Board member Thomas held up a hand to signal for Reverend to hold his commentary.

McLeod resumed, "We have lost an awarding-winning leader, two talented teachers, and now apparently an entire student body. Staying the course should be the last thing we do." Everyone except Thigpen nodded in agreement. "We have to restore confidence in our school or else we won't have a school."

Cluelessly, Van Vetchen inserted, "We'll have a school. Where else will they go?"

If looks could kill, then the laser-like eye daggers from the other four board members would have sliced Van Vetchen into pieces. Even more than they hated her privileged perspective, they hated the morsels of truth within her statement.

Without sensitivity, Van Vetchen continued, "They left Detroit Public Schools. What other options do you people have?"

This time McLeod stood up and spoke with sinister deliberation, "Watch your damn mouth."

Thomas inserted himself, "We have a responsibility to these children, let's get to it. One of us should contact the staff and find out what's going on. Then we can all start alerting parents about when school will restart."

Everyone knew that Thomas was right.

Four of them pondered Reverend's delusional ministry.

Three of them knew that should they right these circumstances, they would eventually need to replace two board members.

Two of them contemplated ways to blame Principal Robeson.

One of them knew the truth; without Robeson, Ella Baker was on a fast track of decline.

None of them knew what would happen next.

39

IT MAKES ME WANNA CRY

Mavis Staples

Friday, February 7, 2014

"I'll be damned if this aint deja-vu," Francine whispered sadly as Joyce and Elaine made their way over to her booth at the Roostertail restaurant. When they got closer she asked, "Cleve ain't gonna be too upset with me for intruding on y'all's skating is he?"

Elaine responded, "He said you're good for this one time, but don't make it a habit."

They shared a short laugh but the somber undertone in Francine's laughter caused Elaine and Joyce greater worry.

"Well, out with it Francine. What's so urgent we got to drop what we're doing and see you?"

Francine took a deep breath while taking in the view of the Detroit River. This view adds a touch of elegance to the Roostertail experience. She acquiesced, "I got a big meeting on Monday."

The statement confused her friends.

Joyce nearly stuttered as her fears began to get the best of her, "Wh-what type of meeting?"

"The ole Emergency Manager say they been reviewing contracts and want to ask me some questions."

This time all of them took in the view of the river.

Forty-five years ago, they shared a similar somber moment that found them staring out into the distance.

Friday, February 7, 1969

"Francine, it's too cold for any bullshit. Why we gotta meet you out here?" Elaine asked with agitation.

This 9:00 pm meeting at the Fountain at Wilberforce University was an outdoor meeting, in central rural Ohio, in February - only the best of friends would endure that type of cold.

Joyce's teeth were already chattering as she and Elaine had hurried over from Henderson Hall.

"I can't have babies."

"What?! You brought us out here to tell us that?" Elaine nearly screamed.

"I'm pregnant and I can't go home with a baby."

Both Joyce and Elaine's jaws dropped as they processed the stunning news.

"How did you get pregnant?" Joyce asked.

Elaine and Francine stared at her stupidly. She tried to clean it up, "I mean what you doing getting pregnant? We came here to learn not become parents."

"Thanks Joyce, that's good to know."

Elaine slid her arm over Francine's shoulder as she stood next to her. "What are you thinking about doing?"

They waited several seconds before the words formed on Francine's tongue.

"I'm gonna get an abortion."

"WHAT!"

"You're gonna kill the baby!"

"It's either that or my mama kills me. Plus, I only missed two periods so it can't really be a real baby yet."

Both Joyce and Elaine reluctantly agreed.

"Where are you gonna get the abortion done and how are you going to pay for it?"

"I don't know yet. I mean, that's why y'all here. Y'all 'spose to fill me in on those things."

"We don't know nothing about no abortions!"

Joyce elaborated, "Except one thing; sometimes things go wrong, and the woman can't get pregnant again."

"So, you telling me either get killed by my mama or maybe, just maybe never have kids?"

"Nawl, girl that's not what I'm saying. I'm saying, well, you know ..." Joyce shushed herself.

That night, three girlfriends sat in the freezing cold, staring into the distance and facing a choice that had no appealing options.

Friday, February 7, 2014

"THEY ARE GOING TO PRESS CHARGES AGAINST YOU, IF ONLY for the spectacle of it," Joyce shared.

"But I ain't did nothing nobody else wasn't doing," Francine declared unconvincingly.

Elaine just sighed and ran her hands over her head.

Secretly, she recognized once again the benefit of the support system she had as a beginning teacher. Her principal, Mrs. Payne, was a tough but by-the-book leader. Francine on the other hand, experienced a quick career ascent from teacher, to lead teacher, to department leader, to assistant principal, and eventually, principal. Her mentor and sugar daddy, Mr. Hollins, was a known womanizer and his public outings with Francine undermined her qualifications for each of those roles. No one saw her talent for leadership. They only saw her as sexing her way to the top. But worse than that perception, was the skimming money habit she learned from Hollins.

Years of a nickel and dime here and there had evolved into a couple hundred here and a few thousand there. Both Elaine and Joyce long suspected the source of Francine's extra income but never confronted their friend for fear of learning the truth. They knew what a principal's salary was and it did not afford the lifestyle Francine lived.

This was worse than the night at the Fountain.

"So, you're going to fight these allegations, right?" Elaine asked, while hoping that Francine's response would prove her innocence.

Francine sipped her wine and stared at Elaine. A few seconds passed before she volunteered, "Elaine, you had something to fight for. What can I win? A reduced sentence?"

"They talked about pressing charges!" Joyce nearly shrieked. After another long sip, Francine responded, "Not yet, they want to see me squirm."

They all sighed and accepted the rough road ahead.

40

I'M STILL IN LOVE WITH YOU

Al Green

Friday, February 14, 2014

*S*tokely and his childhood friend, Wes, were celebrating with a late lunch at Starter's Bar & Grill.

As the newest employee of the Metropolitan Revitalization Organization, Stokely led his first presentation for a group of environmentalists earlier that morning. His ideas were both innovative and fiscally sound. His expertise and confidence won over a group of skeptics, who engaged in post-presentation banter nearly two hours after he concluded. He was nervous when the woman whom he was warned would be the most difficult and cynical, held his arm and laughed loudly at his somewhat funny jokes. She stroked his biceps like he was a kitten, while emphasizing how she was impressed with his vision and detail for adding fitness friendly walkways to downtown Detroit.

His nervousness stemmed from the comment she made before correcting herself. A handful of guests and two board members were talking over hors d'oeuvres when she said, "I just had this vision of you..." while holding her hands up with palms facing each other, shoulder width apart, and her mouth opened in a wide gasp. When everyone looked on in surprise, she clapped, laughed, and corrected herself by saying, "Oh my God, I meant I share your vision. I really see how we can improve Detroit." That's when she latched onto his arm.

WES DOUBLED OVER IN LAUGHTER WHEN STOKELY RETOLD the encounter while they split an appetizer sampler and drank a few beers. The presentation was a good omen for Stokely's future with his new employer and the impromptu celebration with his childhood friend added to his festive spirit. Amid their joviality, Stokely excused himself from the bar to answer a call from his father.

Stokely: "Hey Dad! What's up?"

Cleve: "How did the thing go with them tree- huggers today?"

Stokely: "Dad, man. I killed them. They went from hugging trees to hugging me!"

Cleve: "My man, that's how you do it!"

If voices over the phone could form a high five, then it would have happened right then.

Cleve: "Lookahere, the old boy need you to shoot him a play."

Stokely: "Yeah, cool. Whatcha need?"

Cleve: "I'mma need you to scoop yo' mama up from Joyce's school. I took her car in to the shop and they running late. I thought I'da been outta here, but they still trying to sell me shit."

Both of them laughed.

Stokely: "What time do I need to get her?"

Cleve: "I told her I'd be there by 5:00 so if you can make it happen by then, that would be the move."

Stokely: "Done. I'll holla at you tonight."

Cleve: "Alright, be easy on them tree-huggers. I heard they give recycled Valentine's if you know what I mean."

They laughed some more before hanging up.

"Wes, man, I gotta cut out. That was my old dude. He need me to pick up my Ma." They exchanged an intricate handshake, semi-shoulder hug, and fist pound before splitting up.

When Stokely stepped outside to Plymouth Ave, he saw a vendor selling huge teddy bears and other Valentine trinkets out of the side of a rusted, dilapidated van. It was a reminder that he didn't have a Valentine and a piercing went through his spirit as he made his way to his truck.

CONSIDERING HOW LONG HIS MOTHER AND JOYCE HAD BEEN friends, Stokey's walking into the middle of the conversation being held in Joyce's office would not have been a first. It was like numerous times before. In fact, as he approached the office, he recalled how his mother and her friends would stay after school talking long after the work day was over.

He had been contemplating that thought since he parked in front of the school. He didn't see many cars and he especially did not see a peculiar banana yellow Jeep with oversized tires parked in the rear of the school. Had he seen that Jeep, maybe he could have prepared himself. Maybe he would not have entered the school. He certainly would not have been as shell-shocked as he was when he entered the office.

In a spirit of juvenile silliness, he jumped in the doorway with his arms spread open and yelled, "HAPPY VALENTINE'S!"

His mother laughed, "Oh Stokely!"

And the other person in the office, Phoenix, turned slowly to face what she thought was a familiar voice.

When the woman whose back was to the door turned to face him, Stokely's jaw dropped further than the tree-hugging, arm-holder's did earlier that day.

Phoenix recognized the voice and heard Elaine's response.

With the suddenness of overwhelmed emotion, Phoenix was ejected from her seat and into Stokely's open arms as if it were a natural impulse.

With the familiarity of lovers, Stokely wrapped his arms around her and cradled her head to his chest.

Elaine was blushing harder than forty-something-year old Black women with front row seats at a New Edition concert.

Phoenix and Stokely then shared the most passionate kiss of their relationship. Elaine was doing the happy-faced, teary-eyed, silent clap thing women do, when Joyce walked-in and said, "OOOOHHH!!! Cupid is all up in here!"

They stopped kissing and alternated smiling and hugging each other. Eventually, Elaine inserted, "Stokely, you can turn her loose, she can't get out here." The irony of her statement didn't escape Phoenix or Stokely who were otherwise so enraptured with each other, it was almost as if they were in the room alone.

"Thanks for saving my father," Phoenix whispered.

Stokely nodded "Yes' as he pulled her in for another hug.

"Phoenix, I wish all of that, you know, us meeting everybody and stuff ..." he was reaching for words as the fear of her escape was a potent recurring nightmare. "Look, I just, um, just wish you didn't have to go through that." He leaned his forehead against hers and whispered, "I'm sorry that you had to go through that, I never ..."

Phoenix placed her index fingers on his lips, stood on her tip toes and gave him another kiss.

. . .

Joyce added, "I don't know how Cleve is going to top this Valentine's gift." Both she and Elaine laughed and eased their way out of the office.

"I missed you ..."

They kissed again before Phoenix buried her face between the zipper of Stokely's opened jacket. She began whimpering, which made Stokely pull her closer. When he leaned his face into her hair, the smell brought back the sweetness memories.

"I don't want be away from you ever again ..."

41

MEETING IN THE LADIES ROOM

Klymaxx

Sunday, February 14, 1982

They held their summit in the ladies room of Carl's Chop House. Elaine, Joyce, and Francine had left their husbands and date at the dining table while they conducted their sister-to-sister moment in the restroom.

"What in the hell is wrong with you!" Elaine nearly screamed.

Joyce was right on her heels as she almost shouted, "Francine, that man is married! Why did you invite us on a date with him? If you want to do your thing with married men, do not include us!"

Francine rolled her eyes. "Stanley warned me of jealous people. I just never thought it would be my sister friends," she said in contempt.

"JEALOUS! Ain't nobody jealous of your narrow ass!" Elaine said as Joyce restrained her.

"You are too. Both of y'all. Ever since Stanley gave me my ring, y'all been jealous." Francine folded her arms with the diamond ring on magnificent display as her hand gripped her bicep.

"Don't nobody give a shit about your damn ring. Especially from a fool that's married." Elaine declared. "M-A-R-R-I-E-D, married." Her chest was heaving in anger.

Joyce added, "C'mon Francine, we all know you been sleeping with him but going out in public with him like you are his wife? That's a new low."

"He ain't gonna be married to her much longer. He told me yesterday that he talked to his lawyer and their drafting the divorce papers as we speak."

"You believe that bullshit?"

"Hell Francine, even if you did, out of respect for another woman - wait until the divorce is final before peacocking your ass around town with him. Shit, ain't you ever heard of discretion?"

"Look, when I see what I want, I gets it. I don't pussyfoot around talking about it. I GO GET IT."

"Francine, what the hell you gonna do with that old-ass, married man?! Hunh, he about two years away from geriatric care. How does he even get it up as feeble as he is?"

"Y'all don't need to worry how he gets it up. That's my speciality, gettin' it up. And when the feeling hits me, I get him up and he spits it out, if you know what I mean." Francine smirked before adding, "Maybe y'all don't, considering y'all probably missionary position y'alls men to death."

Joyce and Elaine exchanged confused looks.

CLEVE AND EARL HAD KNOWN EACH OTHER FOR YEARS. They also knew that Francine was the wild child of the trio of friends. Both men had confided in each other how they had to spurn Francine's advances. But tonight's couples date with a married dude was on a whole 'nuther level of Francine's selfishness.

Stanley took a shot at conversation with the others, "Seems like that rookie, what's his name, you know for the Pistons?"

Cleve answered, "Isaiah Thomas."

Stanley continued, "Yeah, Isaiah Thomas. He's pretty good. Coach Knight did a good job with him at Indiana."

Earl chimed in, "He was good without Coach Knight. Coach Knight is alright, but I wouldn't act like he made Isaiah or nothing. The boy is naturally talented with the heart of a lion."

Cleve joked, "More heart than the Detroit Lions."

All the men laughed. It was their diversion from the elephant in the room.

"WE'RE GOING HOME! I CAN'T BE OUT HERE SUPPORTING you with Stanley. Did you forget we know his wife?" Elaine reminded Francine.

"Yeah, yeah" Francine declared in defiance.

Joyce added, "People get killed over this shit Francine. First, you were flirting with him. Then you start fucking him after school. Now this? This is how we get a man nowadays?"

"Fucking? Well, well Joyce, I'm surprised at your language. We only fuck sometimes and the other times we make love."

"That's bullshit. You don't love that man. You love what he can do for you ..."

"Yes, he fucks me well!"

"Before or after you resuscitate his feeble ass?"

Francine rolled her eyes and turned away.

Elaine stormed from the restroom.

She returned to the table as the men discussed how many more terms Coleman Young would serve as mayor.

"Earl, Stanley, please excuse us. I forgot that babysitter couldn't stay late tonight so me and Cleve need to leave.

The men glanced around at each other confused.

Cleve was slow, but he caught on. He snapped his fingers "Yeah, she did say she couldn't stay as long as usual." He bumped his palm against his head for an added affect. "Alright Earl, I'll catch up with you later. Stanley, take it easy."

With that, Elaine nearly snatched him away from the table. Cleve was wise enough to know Elaine's anger wasn't toward him, but if he said or did something wrong, then that dump truck of emotions was going to dump all over him. Knowing that, he hurried behind his wife.

They were headed out the door as Joyce approached the table to leave with Earl.

With their sudden departures, Stanley would have his young mistress to himself, just as he preferred.

42

LET'S CHILL

Guy

Sunday, February 16, 2014

"So, this is the new apartment?" Phoenix asked upon entering.

"Yeah," Stokely replied more dryly than he intended. "I was kind of thinking I would downsize. Sort of get to the essentials and then build back up better."

Phoenix nodded in agreement while processing the meaning of Stokely's downsizing and goal of building back up.

"Care for a drink?"

"That's cool. What do you have?"

"A couple of smoothies from Whole Foods, some water, and grapefruit juice."

Phoenix looked at him for a moment and burst into laughter.

"Stokely, honey ... look, one day I'll show you how to grocery shop."

"What you mean? I know how to grocery shop." He open the fridge and pointed, "See I got eggs, shredded cheddar cheese, eight apples, a couple of kiwis, deli-sliced turkey, and wheat bread!"

Phoenix raised both her hands and wiggled her fingers, "Whhhhoooaaaa, now THOSE are groceries!"

Stokely's pride diminished as he realized she was mocking him.

"But I'd love one of the smoothies."

She said it with a coo, which put a smile back on Stokely's face.

"LET'S TRY SOMETHING," STOKELY SAID AS HE REACHED FOR her hand.

He walked her over to the center of his studio apartment and told her to have a seat on the floor.

She was confused.

He sat first and opened his legs into a V.

He pulled her down until she sat with her bottom near the intersection of his V. Her feet were flat on the floor and her knees bent just behind Stokely's shoulders.

She leaned back, but Stokely pulled her closer.

"This isn't foreplay."

"Ooookkaaayyy. What are we doing?"

"We're talking. Heart to heart. Me and you."

"Alright." She waited a moment. "Ok, hi."

"Hi Phoenix."

"This is weird."

"Ask me something?"

"Did you do this with Tanya?"

"I hope that wasn't the hard question," Stokely chuckled. "No, this is new. Between me and you."

Phoenix nodded a slow yes, with an 'Okay' stuck between her pursed lips.

"Where do you see yourself in five years?"

"These questions getting easier," Stokely smiled, which made Phoenix blush. "Coming home to you."

Phoenix's eyes widened.

"You do know I'm not the stay-at-home type."

"The rapport you have with my mom told me that."

"Yeah, let's talk about your mom."

"Okay."

"She's cool."

"Cooler than a fan."

"I heard about her troubles at the school, but when I met her, I didn't put two and two together you know?"

Stokley nodded.

"Plus, she introduced herself as Mrs. Elaine."

"She knew who you were because I showed her that picture you sent me."

"You told your mother about me?"

"You told your mother about me, remember? Y'all even had me in church."

Phoenix laughed as she recalled Stokely's response to visitor's welcome. She said, "Remember in *Coming to America* when Prince Akeem stands suddenly and shouts, 'I'm very happy to be here!'"

Stokely was embarrassed, "I ain't look that silly, did I?" He placed his hand over his face.

"You were cute though." Phoenix recalled something else. "You said I was your girlfriend."

"Yeah, I did." Stokely was looking around shyly. "I was trying to speak it into existence, sort of, kinda like ..."

Phoenix took a sip of her smoothie and offered some to Stokely. He sipped. After which she used her finger to wipe the remaining smoothie from his lips. Then she licked her finger.

"You trying to seduce me?"

"You won't have to wonder should the situation ever arise."

"Should I continue to speak you being my girlfriend into existence?"

"Couldn't hurt."

"You leaving again, that would hurt."

She place her finger on his lips to shush him.

"Tell me something good that doesn't have to do with us."

Stokely's face brightened, "Song will be paroled!"

"YES!! That's awesome!!"

"I'm going to pick her up Wednesday!"

"I bet your parents are excited."

"They don't know yet. The previous times Song went before the parole board and was denied, my parents were crushed. So, this time, we ain't saying nothing until she steps through the front door."

"They're going to be overjoyed."

"Me too." Stokely's eyes wandered away as he pondered, "My big sister is coming home, wow."

"I can't wait to meet her. And your dad too."

"Yeah, I look forward to that."

"I was about to say you met my whole family, but let's stop there. I'm not ready to think about you and my dad."

"On to the next thing."

Phoenix extended her pinkie to him. He hooked his with hers.

"Stokely, I like the idea of being your girlfriend." She was smiling. "I even like the idea of you coming home to me."

Stokely was smiling.

"I'm still kinda shook over the Auto Show, you know?"

"Yeah."

"So, I pinkie swear to work through it with you without blaming you."

Stokely tightened his pinkie hook, "Count me in."

She caressed his faced and kissed him slowly.

"I look forward to our next heart-to-heart." She then sprang to her feet.

"Are you picking up your mother this week?"

Stokely didn't want her to go, but appreciated the pinkie swear.

"If it means I'm going to see you; yeah, I'm going to get her every day."

With her purse over her shoulder, she walked back, bent over, and kissed Stokely on the forehead.

"So, you want to see me every day, hunh?"

"And every night."

"Hmmmmm. Maybe we'll get there." She bit her lip as she imagined that reality.

"But not tonight."

"Facetime me tonight, okay?"

She was headed to the door as Stokely meekly replied, "Okay."

When she held the door and smiled back at him, she added, "I hope this isn't the last time you ask me over."

She closed the door behind herself before he could reply.

He leaned back, laid on the floor, and thanked the ancestors for Phoenix's return.

43

JOYOUS FLAME

Googie & Tom Coppola

Wednesday, February 19, 2014

*T*hey ran into each other's embrace as soon as the gate opened.

The twenty years of distance did not diminish the love between brother and sister. When Songhai began her prison sentence, Stokely was an adolescent boy angered by the unfairness his sister's future held. As he grew into manhood, he experienced a spectrum of emotions regarding his sister's penal sojourn - everything from resentment to bitterness, from hopelessness to irrational optimism, and from daily prayers to doubting the divine.

However today, joy is the over-riding emotion.

Songhai had witnessed her brother's growth into manhood with each visit. Today, after all that time with women, she welcomed masculine security. For the first time in many years, she felt safe. She did not say so, but she saw in her brother, a strong resemblance to their father as she remembered him back when she was a little girl. Running into Stokely's embrace was just like four-year-old Songhai running to Cleve for him pick her up and swing her around.

She felt that safe. She felt loved.

"Ma and Dad are going to faint when you walk through the door!" Stokely shouted with glee as he opened the door for his sister to get inside his F150. The passenger seat was the most comfortable seat Song had in years. She buckled herself in as a safety precaution, not against other drivers, but sort of a stabilizing force for the enormity of emotions welling up inside her.

Stokely jumped in the driver seat and just stared at his sister. His smile was warmer than the summer sun. He reached for her hand and rubbed it with both of his. He kept repeating her name in a soft sing-song manner, "Song, Song, Song …"

Her naturally fiery red hair had dulled a bit. Grey hair was interspersed throughout her cornrowed mane. Her orangish skin and freckled face seemed to brighten with a happiness that reflected Stokley's smile and manifested her own innate warmth.

Finally, Stokely declared, "I guess we should head home." His smile intensified.

"Home," Song whispered in disbelief. "We're going home, Stokely. Let's go … home?"

Neither of them could hold back the tears.

A penitentiary patrol car honked for them to get moving and compelled Stokely to finally put the truck in gear.

CLEVE WAS DOING A RAGGEDY-ASSED TWO STEP DANCE AS HE prepared dinner.

Elaine had piled a week's worth of laundry onto the sofa and was folding clothes while intermittently joining Cleve in duets playing from the cassette tape deck he'd mounted in the kitchen decades ago.

"It still works!" was his defense against removing the artifact from their kitchen. Elaine had long accepted if the tape deck and off-key singing that accompanied it facilitated his preparation of dinner, then it could certainly stay.

"Looks like Stokely pulling in the driveway," Cleve shouted from the kitchen while using a spatula as a microphone and doing his best Solomon Burke imitation.

"I think he got Little Honey Dip with him. Looks like. I don't know. Didn't you say she was short?"

"Cleveland, I did not. I said she reminded me of a gymnast."

They were both laughing when Stokely opened the door, shouted "SURPRISE!", and stepped aside to reveal Songhai standing in the doorway.

Both Cleve and Elaine were frozen with joyous disbelief. As if they were beholding a lovely apparition, they looked at each other and then simultaneously shouted, "SONG!!!"

Stokely couldn't remember seeing his parents move so fast. Cleve spread his arms wide enough to engulf the entire clan in his embrace. Elaine squealed with exhilaration, "My baby is home!! Song, come here! OOOoooooohhhh baby Song!!" Cleve rocked the family in a rhythmic love hug.

They stood there together for many minutes basking in the bliss of answered prayers and showering themselves with tears of joy. It took the shrill alarm of the smoke detector going off in the kitchen to snap them from their happiness trance.

44

SITTIN' UP IN MY ROOM

Brandy

Thursday, February 20, 2014

*L*ast night's burned dinner was replaced by pizza.

After Stokely bid the family 'good night' and Cleve ventured to bed, Elaine had Song sit on the floor between her legs. Elaine's maternal instinct showed no rust as she went to work on taking down Songhai's cornrows. Elaine saw her daughter's cornrows as emblematic of the restraints of prison. The absence of sheen and the abundance of dandruff reminded Elaine that survival was the primary self-care option in prison.

They did not communicate with many words but love and care were being communicated in abundance.

Although Elaine said it aloud, she was really talking to herself when she stated, "I've been wearing my hair short for a while, but I still got the goods to take care of you."

Her next statement was a directive for Song, "Go on and pull up a chair to the kitchen sink. I'm gonna get my shampoo, conditioner, and blow-dryer. Then we can get you right."

All the events of the evening were heartwarming and

restorative for Song. However, it wasn't until the cool water rushed over her scalp, her mother's fingers did their scratchy dance all over her head, and the sweet scent of coconut oil shampoo wafted into her nostrils that the magnitude of really being home set in for Song.

It wasn't unusual for Cleve to awaken around 2:30 am. It was as if he slept in two four-hour shifts with a break in between. As he made his way down the hall, he saw the light in Song's bedroom and said a short prayer of gratitude before leaning quietly in the doorway.

Elaine preserved their daughter's bedroom as it was in 1994. The huge *What's the 411?* poster featuring Mary J. Blige still overlooked the full-sized bed. The small jewelry box still contained the gold necklace with Song's name affixed to it along with three of those rings with the little spin-around things on them. A four-foot-tall Winnie-the-Pooh bear remained in the sentry position in the corner where the head-rest met the wall.

Songhai sat at the edge of the bed with slumped shoulders while staring at her framed acceptance letter to Spelman College.

The baritone of Cleve's voice gave his whisper a rumble as he approached her from behind, "Soooooonnnggg." As was his custom when he would awaken her as a child, he used his thumb and pointing finger to rub the lob of her ear. "I see yo' mama got your hair looking all good and fresh." Her orangish skin moved up a notch in radiance.

Cleve went over to the wall, placed his back against it, and slid down. All of the Robeson's knew that this was Cleve's heart-to-heart,   I'm-bracing-myself-for-what-could-be-a-tough-conversation position. The last time these two faced each other in this way, Cleve did not manage to ask if Song was sexually active, but he talked about how beautiful love-making can be with people who loved each other. He stressed immature boys who didn't really know what they were doing while getting their rocks-off was not often pleasant for the girls. Thankfully, Elaine was his teammate and got to the bottom of that conversation.

Now finally, here they were again, but Cleve anticipated this conversation would be more important and significantly easier.

"You know we use picture frames to capture a moment in time."

Song smiled as she remembered her dad's tendency toward parables. She nodded in agreement.

"But what would be unfair to everyone was if we got frozen in those moments, you know what I mean?"

She nodded again.

"Thangs changed as they often do and shit doesn't always go as planned." He paused before cautiously proceeding, "But, that smart and ambitious girl that got accepted to Spelman is now a smart and ambitious woman." He bit his lip with a bit of uncertainty as he continued, "That acceptance letter there," he placed his finger on the edge of the frame. "It is just a memorial to what we always knew." He took a deep breath, "Now we gonna go forward with those truths we've known all along."

Song replied, "Daddy, I feel like such a waste."

"Shit nawl, you ain't no waste. You went through all that for a reason. A reason we gotta learn, but a reason neverthe-less." He was aware that this was a very sensitive time. He proceeded cautiously, "That time away is a part of your story; it ain't your whole story, just a part."

A minute or so passed before he shifted the conversation. "Song, truthfully, the ole boy need a little help." Song was confused but recognized that when Cleve shifted to third person, he was being vulnerable. "Er'y now and then Stokely come along with me, but it's looking more and more like I need a steady partner." He paused before saying, "Know what I mean?"

"Daddy, I don't know nothing about plumbing."

"You always were a fast learner, though."

Song laughed, "A woman ain't got no place doing plumbing work, Daddy."

"A woman's place is wherever in the hell she wanna be."

Song smiled as she added, "Yeah, I could use a few dollars."

As he rose to kiss her on the forehead, he asked, "Cash or check?"

A few tears escaped Song's eyes.

"Try to get you a little sleep. We gonna swing by the store to get you some work clothes. I'mma let you and yo' mama handle the pretty clothes." He stopped at the door, turned, and said, "Alright partner, we got our work cut out for us." He winked and headed to the kitchen.

That night, Song slept peacefully.

45

WHO IS HE (AND WHAT IS HE TO YOU)?

Bill Withers

Tuesday, February 25, 2014

*O*f all of the responsibilities she had as a principal, Francine's favorite pastime was model teaching a lesson for her beginning teachers. She would walk through the lesson planning with the novice and place emphasis on learning outcomes, how this particular lesson fits where the students need to be in their development, and student time-on-task.

More often than not, teachers would ask about classroom management and though Francine could yell and be intimidating, she stood steadfast by her belief that effective and relevant instruction were the best tools for classroom management. If the students are enthused about learning and know how to proceed, they simply do not have time for anything else.

There were only a handful of veterans left in Detroit Public Schools who knew Francine, Elaine, and Joyce as principals. All would agree that Francine was the best at staff development. They would agree that Joyce's maternal energy gave her an advantage few could replicate. Those veterans would also say that Elaine would be the result if one took the best attributes of Francine and Joyce and merged them into one. But Elaine's Achilles' Heel was following leaders that she did not respect, which turned out to be a recurring pothole in her career path.

Francine, they would say, tended to have a different rapport with her leaders, especially the men.

Francine's alleged home wrecker reputation was almost mythological. Francine was of the mind that if people feared her then they would respect her. Many women feared leaving their man around Francine, but none more than Ethel Hollins, wife of the late Stanley Hollins.

Ethel was old school and did not believe in divorce. She had long known Stanley was a wandering-eye philander; but when he got wrapped up in Francine Franklin, Ethel knew she had lost her husband. They remained married in title only. He relished her protest of sleeping in another room. He ignored her empty threats of leaving. He laughed off her accusations of spending money on that hussy - even though he had a joint bank account with Francine.

The same bank account that drew two red flags from the Emergency Manager: why was a deceased employee still on payroll and who was cashing the checks?

Mercifully, Ethel passed before Stanley. If she weren't already dead, Francine's arrival at her funeral would have killed her. There was an orchestral rendition of teeth-sucking and deep sighs when Francine arrived to pay her last respects to her former co-worker. Stevie Wonder and the Five Blind Boys of Alabama could see through Francine's charade of grief. And all could see what a spectacle Stanley's life had become.

When Stanley showed Francine a strategy of over-billing the district and splitting the difference between herself and the respective vendor, he found her to be overly enthused with the lesson. His point of scant use and small amounts was ignored. With each year following his death, Francine grew more consumed with money. It filled the empty part of her soul until it became obvious that her ride on the money train was nearing its last stop.

HER INSPIRING MORNING OF MODEL TEACHING WAS followed by a solemn afternoon in the district's main offices. She opted not to bring her attorney for the afternoon meeting with the Emergency Manager and Wellington Shelby. When she arrived at the Midtown conference room, the Emergency Manager led with a peculiar question - "How well did you know the late Stanley Hollins?"

"Back when I taught fifth grade, he was my principal and supervisor."

Wellington added, "Was that all he was to you?"

Francine knew where this conversation was headed but played along for the hell of it. "He was a mentor, role model, and friend."

"How well of a friend?" Wellington asked while relishing the set-up to the big 'aha!'

The Emergency Manager held up a hand.

"Ms. Franklin, we've done our due diligence. We are aware of your history with Mr. Hollins." He looked over his glasses for assurance that she recognized that he did not want to go into details, but would if necessary.

"Okay, you called me down here because I had a crush on my supervisor?"

"Ms. Franklin, I wish it were that simple; however, it is not."

"Well ... whatcha got?"

"Direct connections to three vendors with a history of

overcharging the district for supplies and a paper trial that is leading us to another."

"Y'all say that to everybody."

"We do?" Wellington and Emergency Manager replied.

"That's what I've been hearing. Y'all trying to bully folks into working with y'all."

The Emergency Manager shrugged, "Numerous instances of overcharging the district and a history of cashing the checks of a deceased employee - all that sounds like prison time to me Ms. Franklin. What does it sound like to you?"

"Sounds like I'm being framed for shit I didn't do."

The Emergency Manager brought both hands on the table with a gentle pat, pushed away from the table, and extended his hand for a shake. Francine shook his hand very limply while cutting her eyes at Wellington.

"We will be in touch soon."

MR. PITIFUL

Otis Redding

Tuesday, February 25, 2014

*R*everend Amos Thigpen had a thing for the limelight. Somehow, some kind of way, he made some type of television appearance each week. He lacked the panache to be even be a poor man's Al Sharpton, but he definitely was compelled by a bulldogged persistence.

A persistence that outlasted the other members of the Ella Baker Academy School Board.

JOYCE, ELAINE, PHOENIX, AND CYNTHIA WERE WRAPPING-up a long and productive day that included introducing BBD to the Tubman Technical Academy Parent Teacher Association. They were sharing laughs and high-fives when they entered the office in time for the six o'clock news. The secretary was watching TV and was about to turn it off until Elaine turned ashen white as if she seen a ghost. Reverend Amos Thigpen was front and center on the evening news.

Reporter: *Ella Baker Academy is under new leadership. Today after an emergency meeting with the Governor, Ella Baker Academy is now a part of the state-wide Educational Acceleration Association School Reform District. This partnership dissolves the Baker Academy School Board while leaving its Principal Amos Thigpen in place to guide the school to its former glory.*

JOYCE TURNED OFF THE TV.

Phoenix wrapped her arm around Elaine's waist and asked, "Are you going to be okay?"

Cynthia covered her mouth in shock.

"That muthafucka ..." Joyce mumbled under her breath.

"How is the Reverend going to make a deal with the devil?" Elaine asked incredulously. "Since when has this Governor or any Governor gave a shit about the kids in Detroit, hunh?" The question was rhetorical; yet, they all knew the answer. "First, they redirect all the money out of our district, right? Then they create these charter schools. Yeah, we're here and I was there ..." Elaine pointed at the TV, but everyone knew she meant Ella Baker Academy. "And we did, or with y'all, are doing the fucking best we can. But the teacher's union, they got shafted in this whole thing! Now we supposed trust some gotdam Acceleration Association state-wide school board to show us how to teach our kids? THAT'S BULLSHIT!!"

Elaine stormed out of the office.

Joyce ran behind her. She caught her in the main corridor and wrapped her arms around her. All the things Elaine said were true; but Joyce knew that the idea that Thigpen was having the last laugh burned her friend the most.

Elaine was immersed in tears of frustration. "We've given our lives to teaching kids and doing something positive in this damn city and that asshole got the audacity to be up there grinning and skinning with the Governor? He don't give a shit about us and they damn sure don't give a shit about the kids."

Elaine bit her lip hard. "The kids, Joyce - when is somebody gonna give a shit about them?"

"Right now, Elaine. Me and you. Phoenix and Cynthia. My Staff, your staff - we're in the trenches and we give a shit."

Elaine began wiping her tears while listening.

"Thigpen is a megalomaniac who is kissing that white man's ass so that he can rule over us."

"Yeah, I know. History is full of those types; yet and still, like our ancestors - we gotta press forward." Joyce said in a consoling tone. "Elaine, we got two go-getters in that office right now. Two difference-makers. Me and you, we invest in them. We coach and develop them. That's how we win this thing. That's how we save the kids."

Elaine looked at her friend with broken-spirited doubt. "Joyce, I'm tired of always fighting shit that don't have nuthin' to do with education. This shit is politics and bullshit."

Joyce nodded, "You're right." She stepped back. "Where we at? Right now, where are we?"

"Joyce, c'mon. We're at your school ..." Elaine caught it. "Named after Harriet Tubman."

"Yep. Don't you think Sister Harriet had to wade through her share of bullshit and scared negroes?"

Elaine chuckled, "But she would shoot'em if they got out of line."

Joyce laughed, "I know that's right."

They hugged again.

Joyce guided Elaine back toward the office. Phoenix and Cynthia were standing near the doorway with worried expressions. Joyce pointed ahead, "Those two? That's our double-barreled shotgun. They're our shot at the future."

THE WHOLE TOWN'S LAUGHING AT ME

Teddy Pendergrass

Saturday, March 15, 2014

*A*fter she hung up from the call on Friday evening, she commenced drinking. She drank and drank and drank. With each sip of the glass, she inched deeper into caliginous depression.

Francine's years with Detroit Public Schools had afforded her a few friends. One of whom was privy to the inside strategies of the Emergency Manager's Office. One of the strategies was a part of a larger to plan to discredit current school leaders by emphasizing a few unethical ones in the media. The series of discrediting strategies were to commence on Monday morning when the Emergency Manager, Wellington Shelby, the Detroit Police Department, and the local media were going to stage an arrest of Francine at her school.

The plan was to arrest four principals around the city and offer it as evidence that the Emergency Manager was committed to righting the district's wrongs. Such a plan, if executed effectively, would solidify public confidence and allow the Emergency Manager, and indirectly, the Governor to run Detroit Public Schools as they saw fit. On the surface it appeared to be a vigilant effort to save the kids, but beneath the surface it was the removal of millions of dollars from local control into the hands of others.

While Francine's list of crimes were not the worst, they were the most salacious. A long-term sexual affair with a supervisor, cashing a deceased employee's checks, and a history of pilfering that spanned over a decade - all added up to sensational media stories. Francine would be the star of the show!

But, Francine did not want to be that kind of star; although throughout her life, she wanted to be seen.

A montage of memories began flooding Francine's mind as she grabbed her car keys and headed to her garage.

When she opened the car door, she was flooded with memories of local talent shows where kids from her neighborhood would perform and some would eventually sing with Motown. Oh, how she wished she could sing so that she could sign with Motown. But neither Motown nor any of the cute boys at the talent shows noticed her.

When she plopped down into the driver's seat of her car, she recalled how as girl she was playfully bouncing up and down on Uncle Robert's lap. The playfulness of childhood evolved into the nightmares of adolescence as Uncle Robert began to molest her. There was no way to let her mother know. Her mother was trying to save her only brother from the hell heroin addiction was pulling him into. Francine's mother saw in her brother, a family member who would keep the apartment safe while she worked longer hours. Francine experienced a dearth of personal safety while being subjected to Uncle Robert's pedophilic whims.

Francine did not open the garage door. She cranked the

motor and let the car run as if she were warming it up. Her spirits warmed a bit as she thought of her friends, Joyce and Elaine. They had been through a lot together and while she had not always been the best friend to them, they were the closest thing to a family she had. They were going to be disappointed when they saw the news. Especially after what Elaine has been through. During that whole trial she was being compared to some amorphous thief, not realizing that her best friend was the type of thief she was being accused of being.

Francine figured her friends were suspicious but were too caring to confront her. Not that it would have made a difference. In fact, by allowing her to be who she was, Joyce and Elaine were people she grew to trust. Francine closed her eyes knowing that trust would be damaged when they heard the news. Not only Elaine and Joyce, but everyone would know that she was a thief.

A gotdamn thief, what a damn way to be remembered ...

As the car ran and the fumes began to fill the garage, Francine figured all the drinking she had done was catching up with her. She lifted a heavy eyelid and noted that it was 3:13 am on a Saturday morning. Ain't nowhere to go that time of morning. What did the old mens used to say? Yeah, ain't nothin' open that time of night but legs and hospitals. Francine laughed at her own joke. Nothing open this time of night. Nothing open.

Francine's world closed-in as drowsiness engulfed her. That she would die in her car, in her garage, at her house, represented the layers of confinement she felt her whole life. She had been contained by circumstances and personal choices. There was nothing open to her, she had to make her own way on her own terms – even in death.

As she transitioned, her body slumped forward, and her head leaned on the horn. The steady honking of the horn was an announcement to all - move out of the way, Francine was coming through.

FAMILY REUNION

The O'Jays

Sunday, June 1, 2014

*T*hey were walking along a path near Woodward Avenue in Palmer Park.

Stokely pointed across the street to Dutch Girl Donuts. "If people Down South that think Krispy Kreme is the shit had some of the Dutch Girl, they would never want Krispy Kreme again."

"I know that's right," Phoenix agreed.

Then she pointed at the church that was being built on the northeast corner of Woodward and 7 Mile. "When do you think they will finish?"

Stokely shrugged his shoulders, "I don't know. Seems like they've been working on it for a couple of years."

"Yeah, my friend is a member. She says they refuse to go into debt, so they are paying for it as they go."

Stokely pondered the idea, "I like it in principle. But if

new construction is motivation for your membership, then this long-drawn-out construction could be discouraging."

"Yeah, kinda like the long drawn out process of Detroit's comeback."

Stokely shook his head as he processed Phoenix's statement. He was exhaling as he said, "Yyyyeeeahhhh. Detroit is coming back, just slower than we hoped."

"I'll take slow if it equals debt-free."

"This bankruptcy thing - is that a part of the comeback?"

"I don't know, but it's damn sure more discouraging than the drawn-out construction of a church."

This time, Stokely was the one to reply, "I know that's right."

"How's your mom doing?"

"She's holding on. I know she's a warrior and all; but, when I think about her and Aunt Francine, I think that having a family made the difference in her ability to fight or bounce back."

Phoenix nodded her head in agreement.

"Me and my dad, and even Auntie Francine and Auntie Joyce kind of held her down while she was going through that thing with her school board. Then Song coming home, kind of gave her that extra whatever to survive Francine's suicide."

"She told me she needed some time away from the school and BBD. She said it wasn't personal, but she just didn't want to be at any school."

"Damn, she told you that?" Stokely was in shock. "She must REALLY like you."

Phoenix smiled.

"You know what, let's go see her." Phoenix's smile brightened. "My parents don't stay far from here, let's go."

"Let's do it!" Phoenix responded cheerfully.

AFTER THE CHILDREN WERE OUT OF THE HOUSE, CLEVE converted the basement into a storage and work space for his company. They were all down there with Song sitting atop a counter announcing the goals for the week.

"Tomorrow morning, we're going to have to go to Wyoming Plumbing Supply and load up some pipes, two sinks, and a toilet."

Cleve chuckled as he stared at Elaine.

Elaine was seated on a stool. Cleve had his two middle fingers balanced on Elaine's temples. He stared at her closely while shifting his head slightly from side to side. He then, wiped his razor on his shirt before applying it just so to Elaine's head.

"Can't have my baby out here with a crooked line-up," he said to himself. Once Elaine committed to short cropped hair styles, Cleve became her personal barber.

He reached for the mirror and allowed Elaine to inspect his work.

"You want me to go lower or is this about right?"

"Mmmmm, Song, what do you think?"

Song placed her notes aside and hopped down from the counter top and walked over for a closer inspection.

"Daddy, you gotta tighten up over here. It's not as low as the other side."

Song's parents laughed.

Ever since she began working with Cleve, she has made his good work better. While she was slowly getting better as a plumber, her business acumen made Cleve's plumbing services more efficient. Song created a schedule, did inventory, and loaded the truck for parts needed for a given day. She mapped out their jobs while scheduling time for a hearty lunch. With Song, revenue and productivity increased substantially.

This added improvement was one that began spilling over into other parts of Cleve's life. From keeping his doctor appointments, to even Elaine's haircuts, Cleve valued Song's input.

He switch the guard on the clippers and leaned in. Before he could get going, Stokely yelled from upstairs.

"Where y'all at?!"

Their choral reply was, "Downstairs."

Song walked over to the steps to meet Stokely as he descended. They shared a big hug and Phoenix received an even bigger one.

Cleve bellowed, "There she is, Miss Sunshine!"

Phoenix blushed and gave him a hug while Stokely kissed his mother.

"Dad hooking you up?"

"He trying," Elaine teased.

"You want the ole boy to tighten up your fade?" Cleve asked jokingly.

To which Phoenix joined in, "If you don't I will."

Everybody laughed.

"Dang, a brother skip the barber one week and y'all talk bad about him."

Song kept it going, "I mean if yo' mama's hairline is tighter than yours, I'm just saying."

Phoenix high-fived Song.

"Y'all leave my baby alone," Elaine added. "Son, grow that hair while you can ..." Then she looked at Cleve.

"Hey, hey!! What y'all trying to say?!"

"Oh daddy, the George Jefferson hairline looks good on you," Song said as she laughed.

Which prompted Cleve to strut around the basement with the George Jefferson walk.

"Phoenix, honey, how's the program going?" Elaine asked.

"Mrs. Elaine, we got more girls than we planned for! I thought we were just going to do twenty girls two days a week, but we got forty girls on a Monday-Wednesday and Tuesday-Thursday schedule. The feedback is awesome!"

"Joyce ain't getting in the way telling you how to do your thing is she?" Elaine asked jokingly.

"She's fine. She gives me and Cynthia all the space we need to make it do what it do."

"Do what it do!" Cleve shouted. "That's alright." He stepped closer to resume trimming Elaine's hair while asking, "What y'all got going on today?"

"We was in the neighborhood and just dropped by," Stokely responded while grabbing a seat on the bottom stair. Song had resumed her perch on the countertop and Phoenix pulled up a nearby chair.

Cleve took Elaine's head in his right hand and used his left to trim over the uneven spot. He added, "Why don't you go on and pull out the grill so we can fire up some grub."

Song didn't miss a beat, "Yeah, if you cooking. If Stokely cooking, I say we order some food."

Everybody was laughing as Stokely extended his middle finger and attempted to disguise it as a scratch to his beard.

PHOENIX WAS TAKING IT ALL IN, PARTICULARLY CLEVE. HE was unlike any father or husband she had ever seen, and it was easily apparent from whom Stokely learned manhood. She looked again at Mrs. Elaine, who was the happiest Phoenix recalled ever seeing her, despite her friend's death. Then in Song, Phoenix saw the big sister she never had. She also saw Song as beautifully built daughter embodying the resilience she wanted to develop in the girls involved with BBD.

The familial chatter and rounds of laughter among the family brought Phoenix's attention back to Stokely. Denise often told her that the way a man treats his mother and how his father treated the mother are indicators of how that man will treat the women in his life. Phoenix sort of chuckled as she imagined Stokely giving her a haircut, which had to be better than his cooking.

From her perch on the barber stool, Elaine inserted, "Y'all don't worry about cooking, I'll take care of it." Everyone looked on in a bit of surprise and then in a flashback spanning decades, Song and Stokely looked to each other smiling. Just like when they were kids, they prepared to finish what they knew their mother would say next.

Elaine continued, "I'll cook up something so good, it'll be ..."

Song and Stokely gleefully shouted in unison, "... TENDER AS A MOTHER'S LOVE!"

Better Left Unsaid

Assuming Hurts

Listen Up
A Memoir of Perspective

Fred Duncan with Sabin Duncan

Listen Up: A Memoir of Perspective (with Fred Duncan, Jr.)

Reflections from the Frontline

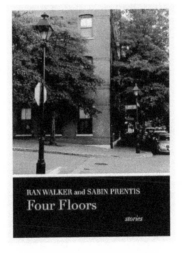

Four Floors (with Ran Walker)

ABOUT THE AUTHOR

Sabin Prentis is a husband, father, educator, native Detroiter, and creator of Literary Soul Food. He is the owner of Fielding Books *and the author of Assuming Hurts, Better Left Unsaid, Reflections from the Frontline,* and co-author of *Listen Up and Four Floors.*

Creative Team

Tiffany L. Hall - Creative Director
Kathryn Hrobowski - Cover Model
George Mitchell - Photographer
Ife Thomas - Audiobook Narrator

For more information:
www.sabinprentis.com